# A HOLIDAY IN EVERY HEART

## AN ENCHANTED LEGACIES CHRISTMAS NOVELLA

# ALSO BY KATE KING

## ENCHANTED LEGACIES

A Thorn in Every Heart

A Storm in Every Heart

A Holiday in Every Heart: An Enchanted Legacies Christmas Novella

## WILDE FAE

Lords of the Hunt

Lady of the Nightmares

The Last Heir of Elsewhere

A Kingdom of Monsters

## THE GENTLEMEN

Red Handed

Thieves Honor

Damned Souls

## THE BLISSFUL OMEGAVERSE

Pack Origin

Pack Bound

Pack Bliss

## STANDALONES:

By Any Other Name: A Deliciously Dark Romeo and Juliet Retelling

ENCHANTED LEGACIES
BOOK 2.5

# A HOLIDAY IN EVERY HEART

## AN ENCHANTED LEGACIES CHRISTMAS NOVELLA

USA TODAY & INTERNATIONAL BESTSELLING AUTHOR

# KATE KING

A Holiday in Every Heart © 2025 by Kate King



First Cover edition November 2025

Barnes and Noble Edition: 979-8-9917934-9-0

Paperback: 979-8-9933495-1-0

Cover design and typography: Flowers and Forensics

Edge Design: Painted Wings Publishing Services

Proofreading: Emily in the Archives @emilyinthearchives

Published by Wicked Good Romance

*To those who need a reminder that
magic still exists after happily ever after*

DYASPORA
THERMIA
VERNALLIS

ELLENDER
N
W
E
S
SOLISTINE
HYDRATTA

# STOP! READ THIS FIRST

A Holiday in Every Heart is not a standalone story. It is essentially a long, extended epilogue, intended as a low-stakes treat for the readers who already know and love the Enchanted Legacies characters and want to know what they're up to between full-length books. AHIEH takes place two years after A Thorn in Every Heart and six months after the events of A Storm in Every Heart. It will ruin the ending of both books.

Every other book in the Enchanted Legacies series can be read and understood independently, so if you are trying out this series for the first time, I recommend starting somewhere else and coming back to this book once you are already familiar with the world.

Happy Holidays and Happy reading!

# A HOLIDAY IN EVERY HEART

ALIX

"Ouch!" I wince and recoil away from the sharp pain stabbing into my side.

The elderly seamstress circling me like a vulture sniffs and throws me a dark look. "Apologies, my lady...but if you would just stop moving..."

I let out a long breath and swallow the retort I'm longing to blurt out. I'm not moving—at least not by human standards. And if I am, it's only because she keeps stabbing me with her damn pins.

"If it helps, you look amazing," Odessa says from where she's leaning against the end of my bed. "You're almost done. Just hold your breath."

I wrinkle my nose, but take her advice and hold my breath as the seamstress adds another row of pins to the waist of my gown.

We're only two days away from my wedding, and I'm

standing on a low platform in the middle of my bedroom, while Dessa supervises the stab-happy Fae seamstress putting the final touches on my wedding gown.

Odessa just arrived in Vernallis this morning, having spent the last several months out at sea with her soul-bond, Kastian, and their new crew. I'd been getting a little nervous that they wouldn't come back in time for the wedding, but I should have known better. Dessa would never want to miss this.

"How are the wishes coming along?" Odessa asks, clearly aiming to distract me.

"We're nearly done. I—"

"Don't talk!" the seamstress hisses, cutting me off as she stabs another pin into my stomach.

I flinch violently again, and my eyes water. "Okay, that's it. I need a break."

The seamstress sniffs with disapproval. "Don't sit down! You'll wrinkle it."

"I won't," I promise. "I just need a five-minute break."

"Fine!" she snaps, throwing her hands up and stepping back. "I'll be back soon."

She wafts out of the room as I step down from the small raised platform and let out a long breath.

Odessa catches my eye and grins. "Nerine is the best seamstress in Ellender, you know...even if she is a little, um, *aggressive.*"

"Oh, I know," I sigh. "Beatrix called in a favor to get her here. Apparently, even a royal wedding wasn't enough of a draw to make her come out of retirement on its own. There was an unfulfilled bargain involved too."

"This is your last fitting; you can do it," she says bracingly. "You know what they say: beauty is pain."

I grimace. "I'm not sure that's supposed to be so literal. Do you really like the dress though?" I twirl in a circle, the skirt fanning out around me.

Fae wedding dresses are gold, not white like human ones, and mine catches the light like a living flame. The short sleeves sweep off my shoulders, and the tight, corseted bodice is embroidered with hundreds of tiny silk flowers, glittering beads, and intricate lace that could be etched from genuine gold. The enormous skirt cascades around me in layers of gossamer fabric so fine that when I move, even slightly, the whole gown shimmers.

"Absolutely," Dessa gushes. "It's perfect. Isn't it, Aurelia?"

We both turn toward where Aurelia is sitting on the window seat across the room. Her knees are pulled up to her chest beneath her long skirt, and she's peering out through a little patch she's rubbed on the frosted glass. She's been so quiet, it was almost as if she wasn't there.

At the sound of her name, Aurelia startles. "Sorry, what did you ask?"

"Just fishing for compliments," I grin. "What are you looking at?"

"Nothing!" she says too quickly, pulling her gaze from the window. "Sorry. Catch me up. What were we talking about?"

"I was asking Alix how the wishes are coming along," Dessa says.

She's wearing black leather pants, tighter than anything I've ever seen her wear before, and her red hair has bleached gold from the sun. She looks like a pirate princess as she sits back down on my bed and crosses her legs.

"Good." I sigh. "Thank God we're almost done, though. If I'd realized how many weird traditions Fae have around weddings, I would have insisted Daemon and I elope."

"Don't let Beatrix hear you say that," Aurelia comments.

"Oh, she's heard it. I threaten to elope at least twice a day lately. I want to get married, but the actual wedding part is turning into a headache."

Neither of them comments on that, probably because they know I'm one hundred percent serious. I was married once before, and I remember that being incredibly stressful, yet a regular human wedding has nothing on the complexity of a royal Fae wedding.

There have been hundreds of things to do, even with an entire staff of servants to help. Every court in Ellender is invited, and the political maneuvering of having so many royals in one place has been a nightmare. Then, there's simple things like decorations and food, which somehow turned into a production fit for, well, a queen.

To complicate things further, there's a Fae tradition that says that when royals get married, we have to grant a thousand wishes to anyone who asks in the week leading up to the wedding. Daemon and I are at 998 wishes and both so exhausted we can barely see straight.

"We only have a couple more wishes to grant, which is good because we need to go to the human world to visit my mother tonight."

Odessa's eyebrows raise. "Why tonight?"

I sigh, shaking my head. "Because it's Christmas Eve."

I have been regretting choosing December 26th as my wedding date since the moment we chose it.

The Fae don't celebrate Christmas, but they celebrate Yule —a similar holiday which lasts twelve days, and reminds me of dark and witchy holiday aesthetic collages I used to see on Pinterest.

When Daemon and I chose the date of our wedding, we'd hoped that the week of Yule would make it easier for all the visiting courts to attend and perhaps we'd have less work to do and more time to focus on our wedding. In reality, it's made things a hundred times more chaotic.

"You're brave to get married this week," the seamstress says, stepping back into the room. "Some might think it was bad luck."

I snort. "Why? Is there another ancient tradition that I don't know about?"

I'm joking...but like, no I'm not. *Please, dear God, no more surprise traditions!*

The seamstress shakes her head, her mouth tight. "No, my lady. Because of the witch, of course."

*Oh sure, of course, how silly of me to forget the witch.*

Aurelia perks up at the window, interest piqued, and tosses her black braid over her shoulder. "What witch?"

Odessa scoffs. "Oh, please. Don't start, Nerine."

My eyebrows raise. "Wait, what are you talking about?"

"It's just an old story to make children behave," Odessa says soothingly. "Don't worry about it."

"It's not a story," the seamstress snaps. "The Yuletide witch is as real as you and I. She sleeps all year and rises only during this week during the darkest part of the year. When she wakes up, she's starving, and she steals children from their beds to eat for her solstice feast."

I glance sideways at Odessa, raising my eyebrows in question. Two years ago, before I was kidnapped by my one-night stand and discovered that magic and Fae exist, I would have immediately written that story off as insane. Now, I've learned to assume anything could be real until it's proven otherwise.

Odessa groans and rubs her forehead. "It's all nonsense. Folktales to keep children from sneaking out on solstice and getting eaten by wolves."

Nerine's eyes bug out of her head. "Believe what you want, but the witch has already been seen this season. My cousin's neighbor's friend saw her. Some say she has eyes black as coal and teeth sharp as glass. She can transform into a hideous beast, and some say—"

"—that she can't cross running water," a lilting male voice interrupts. "Or that she's terrified of bells. Or that she only eats bad children. Depends on who's telling the story."

I spin around, spotting Daemon in the doorway. He's leaning against the doorframe, arms crossed, staring at me. Instantly, all thoughts of witches and legends disappear from my mind.

Daemon and I have been soul-bonded for more than two years, but I swear to God I will never get tired of seeing him. With his lean muscles, chiseled jaw, and flashing green eyes, he's always just as impossibly handsome as he was the first time we met.

I automatically smile at him, only then I remember he's not supposed to see me. I screech and wrap my arms around myself. "Get out!"

Daemon cocks his head, grinning, and his coppery brown hair falls into his eyes. "What's wrong, Peaches? Are you really sick of me already? We haven't even gone through with the wedding."

I double over as if I can hide my dress with my body alone, and Nerine lets out a pained wail and strides out of the room as if she can't bear to see the gown wrinkled for even a moment. I ignore her, eyes fixed on Daemon. "You can't see my dress! Go away!"

"Why can't he see the dress?" Dessa asks.

"It's bad luck!" I hiss. "Get out, get out!"

"Is that a human thing?" Dessa asks, her brow wrinkling. "And you think we're the ones who have weird superstitions."

Completely ignoring my panic, Daemon pushes off the door frame and crosses the room in two strides. He grips my waist and pulls me toward him, kissing me firmly. Instinctively, I reach up, twining my arms around his neck to pull him closer.

"Excuse me," Odessa says after a long moment. "I should not have to watch my brother maul my best friend. Get a room."

"This is our fucking room," Daemons says with half-hearted annoyance. "You get out."

"Yeah, go maul your own bond." I grin. "It's been at least an hour since Kastian got to feel you up. He's probably in withdrawal.

Dessa sweeps toward the door, grinning wickedly. "You know what, maybe I will."

"I guess I'll go too," Aurelia says, rising from the window seat and moving toward the door.

I glance over at her. Her expression is mild, but something in her tone sounds slightly gloomy. I open my mouth to ask if she's okay, but before I can, Daemon recaptures my lips, and I hear the door snap shut.

Daemon kisses me hard and messy, one hand in my hair and the other taking a scenic tour of the small of my back. The gold fabric of my dress crinkles as he slides his hands up my sides, careful not to prick himself on the pins. A tiny moan escapes my lips, and it's honestly a miracle I don't burst into actual flames with how hot my face is getting.

Finally, Daemon pulls back. "I missed you, Peaches."

I sigh. I know what he means. We sleep in the same bed, but I feel like I haven't seen him all week. Between running the court of Vernallis, granting all the pre-wedding wishes, and final preparations for the wedding and the Yule celebrations, we've barely spoken to each other.

"We need a vacation," I comment. "I guess it's a good thing we're taking that honeymoon."

The Fae don't do honeymoons, but when Daemon realized it meant we could leave for several weeks following and not be bothered by anyone, he launched a campaign to convince the entire court that honeymooning was an important cultural practice for humans, and to not do it would offend me beyond repair. I definitely didn't feel the need to correct him.

He hasn't told me where we're going yet—it's a surprise—but I don't even care. We could stay in this room for two weeks and that would be fine, just as long as we don't get interrupted.

Daemon nods fervently. "Two more days. It's the only damn thing I've been looking forward to for months."

"Oh, so you're not excited about marrying me; you're just excited for the honeymoon?" I tease.

He growls low in his throat and nips at my ear. "I keep telling you, we're already bonded. We don't need to get fucking married."

I roll my eyes. He does keep saying that, and I know he means it as a good thing. In Daemon's head, we're already as committed to each other as it's possible to be, and the wedding is just a difficult and expensive complication. I'd probably agree with him, except that we need to get married so I can officially be the queen of Vernallis...and maybe there's a tiny human part of me that wants to be committed in a way that I grew up dreaming about.

Before I can voice any of that, Daemon lifts me, bridal style, and carries me over to the bed.

"Careful," I hiss. "The seamstress didn't even want me

sitting down in case I wrinkled this dress. You're going to ruin it."

"It would be worth it to get to tear it off you," he says, lips brushing against my bare shoulder.

"It would not!" I yelp. "This took months to make. If you ruin it now, we don't have enough time to get another one."

Daemon flashes me a wolfish grin, then moves with deliberate slowness to deposit me onto the mattress. The gold-laced skirt pools around me like a puddle of molten sun. "Fine. Keep it on, then," he purrs.

I open my mouth to protest, but he's already sinking to his knees at the foot of the bed, hands braced on the mattress, eyes never leaving mine as he slides his torso between my legs and then—God. He disappears under the yards of shimmering fabric.

His hands find my ankles and slip upward, tracing a path over my skin, up my calves to my thighs. I feel his lips follow the same path, his breath fanning over me. My pulse jumps when his lips touch the inside of my knee—just a feather-light kiss—and when he drags his tongue up my inner thigh, I gasp, and grip handfuls of my gauzy skirt until my knuckles go white.

I feel Daemon smile against me before he drags the flat of his tongue right over my soaking wet lace panties.

My hips jerk, involuntary, and the friction of the fabric combined with the heat of his mouth just makes everything more intense. The sensation is enough to short-circuit my entire nervous system. Every muscle in my body burns, waiting for the next touch, the next ruthless flick of his tongue.

He alternates between gentle, teasing licks and firmer, more insistent pressure, never letting me settle into any kind of rhythm or sanity. Every time I gasp, he grins broader, like he's collecting all my desperate noises to play back later when I least expect it. I lace my fingers so tight in the gold skirt that my knuckles crack, and my head is already spinning, vision going hazy at the edges.

Daemon hooks his fingers through my panties and yanks them off before pressing another searing kiss to my core.

My legs tremble, my voice comes out in these chopped, staccato moans, and Daemon just hums in approval, the sound vibrating straight through me, and then he flattens his tongue again, right over where I'm practically throbbing for him, and my heart jackhammers against my ribs so hard I'm half convinced I'll pass out before we even get to the main event.

He parts my folds with two fingers, filling me up to the knuckle. The pads of his fingers stroke that place inside with a pressure that borders on sinful, and when his mouth closes over my clit, sucking gently then harder, my knees lock around his head like a vice and I let out a strangled scream.

I know the entire court can hear me, but at this point I'm beyond caring. My body is not my own; it's a live wire, every nerve coiled and sparking.

He doesn't stop even when my entire body shakes, his mouth relentless and hungry, until the coil in my belly finally comes undone and I shout. The aftershocks roll through me in waves, turning my brain and body to mush.

Daemon resurfaces from beneath the dress, face flushed and wild, hair stuck up at odd angles like he's been electrocuted. His grin is both supremely satisfied and absolutely unhinged.

"You're evil," I pant, breathless.

He just grins, kisses the inside of my knee again, and stands up, looming over me. "I'll take that as a thank you."

I wrap my arms around his neck, pulling him down to the

bed, no longer worried about the yards and yards of golden fabric. Daemon captures my mouth again, and I taste myself on his tongue. He reaches for his belt, and I eagerly reach out to help.

A sharp knock sounds on the door, and we both freeze, fingers twisting around his belt buckle.

"Fuck off!" Daemon yells, immediately turning his burning gaze back on me.

"Sorry about this, mate," Kastian's voice calls from the other side of the door. "Wouldn't bother you, but there's a man downstairs insisting on talking to you."

"Tell him to fuck off!" Daemon growls, louder. "Or you deal with it. I'm busy."

"It's about the wishes," Kastian calls back. "You can't ignore him, or it's—"

"Bad luck," I groan out loud, finishing Kastian's thought. "Goddamnit."

"I don't care," Daemon hisses. "We don't need luck. I do need to be inside you in the next five seconds or I'm going to lose my fucking mind."

A desperate whimper escapes my throat. I want that too—more than pretty much anything right now—but the rational part of me knows we can't.

"If Kas is out there, that means he left Dessa long enough to deal with whoever is downstairs. That must mean it's serious."

Daemon scowls, but I can tell he knows I'm right. He groans and rolls to the side and lies flat on his back looking up at the ceiling. "Have I mentioned that we don't need to get married? This wedding seems like it's about everyone except us."

I sit up. "I know. Focus on the honeymoon. Just a couple more days and we'll be alone for two whole weeks."

He looks placated for half a second, then his face darkens again and he swears violently. "Fuck me."

"What's wrong?"

"I've just remembered that we have to go visit your mother this evening."

I frown too. Yeah...I'm not sure it could get worse than that.

DAEMON

I yank the door open so hard it slams against the frame. Outside, Kastian is leaning against the wall waiting for us. He catches my dark gaze and raises his eyebrows in question.

"Don't," I mutter, brushing past him. "I don't want to fucking hear it."

Alix appears in the doorway behind me, now dressed in simple black trousers and a maroon corseted top. She waves at Kastian over my shoulder. "Hey! Did Dessa ever find you?"

He opens his mouth to answer, then catches my dark expression again and closes it. *Smart man.*

I'm perfectly happy for Odessa and Kastian—if I could have chosen anyone to bond with my sister, it would have been him—but I hate knowing the details of their relationship. It's probably a good thing that they can only live on land for half the year, because I would have lost my mind if I had to hear them across the house every night. I especially hate it right now, knowing that other people are fucking under my own roof, but I can't get five minutes alone with Alix.

My fingers twitch at my sides as I march down the hallway. The ghost of Alix's touch lingers on my neck, my collarbone, places we never got to finish exploring.

*Focus on the honeymoon.*

Only two more days and no one and nothing is going to keep me from fucking my wife against every surface and in every position I can think of.

"Sorry, mate," Kastian says again, falling into step beside me.

"We've already granted hundreds of wishes," I grumble. "The entire country has everything they could ever want. What else is there?"

"He didn't say, it just seemed important."

I nod shortly. In theory, I don't actually hate the traditional wish granting. I'm happy to do anything that will make the citizens of Vernallis's lives easier, and the ceremonial wishes just make it easier for those in need to ask for help without feeling guilty or ashamed. Due to this tradition, all the local farmers have new livestock and seeds for next year, the village children got hundreds of new toys, and our soldiers all have new weapons and armor. We've built dozens of homes for the needy, given out money or food to anyone who needed it, and added more stops to our train system.

All of those things are worthwhile projects, and I'm glad to do it…I just don't want to do it right this fucking second.

"It's actually a good thing that someone came looking for us," Alix points out. "We still have two more wishes to grant before tonight."

The stairs creak beneath our feet as we descend to the first-floor entrance hall. Our house, the manor I grew up in, is starting to look more like a palace every day, with extra rooms stacked magically on top of each other. As we pass by a window, I spot the cobblestone side of Aurelia's tower, which stretches toward the clouds, three stories taller than it was last month.

In the span of two years—and especially in the last six months or so—the small, one-road village of Storia has expanded to three times its original size, and our home has grown to match.

We started by building a barracks for our army. Originally, it was meant to sleep fifty men, as we'd assumed that the majority of the army would still live in the main palaces to the south and east of Ellender. That plan failed when we realized that we might not be at war, but being unprepared would put our entire kingdom in danger. Fox began training the army like a well-oiled machine, and we had to expand the barracks, stables and training grounds to accommodate several hundred soldiers at a time.

The next problem was food. An army that large has to eat, so we expanded the lands of local farmers and brought in more livestock. We had to hire more servants to help cook all that food, clean the barracks and take care of the horses, so we added another wing to the manor to house all of them.

Then, all those farmers and servants brought their families, so we had to build a new school for the sudden influx of local children.

*Then,* all the new villagers wanted an official way to request audiences with the king and queen, so we built a new throne room where our modest sitting room used to be. The throne room is enormous, with towering ceilings and high stained glass windows. At the moment, it's decorated for Yule with bows of pine and garlands of dried fruit hanging from every rafter. In just two days, Alix and I will be married in that room, in the same ceremony she'll be officially crowned the queen of Vernallis.

We reach the bottom of the stairs and stand in the entrance hall. I look around, glowering. "Where's the man with the wish?"

Kastian frowns. "I don't know. He was waiting right here. Maybe someone sent him into the throne room already."

I turn toward the enormous closed doors to our left and push them open. Before I can take another step, I hear my name shouted from somewhere in the direction of the kitchen and freeze. *Now fucking what?*

The door to the dining room flies open, and my mother barrels toward us, trailed by a hunched, flour-dusted woman I vaguely recognize as the neighborhood baker. Both their faces are grim.

"What's wrong?" I ask before my mother can speak.

"There's a storm coming," she announces, hands on her hips. "Nobody's going to be able to travel for days once it hits, which means that all the guests from other kingdoms might not get here in time." She gestures to the baker, who looks ready to faint from equal parts terror and social anxiety. "Also, there's an issue with your cake."

Alix groans. "What happened?"

"One problem at a time," I cut in. "Tell us about the storm."

"It's *winter*, which means *snow*," my mother says somewhat frantically. "I knew you should have waited to get married in the spring."

"Last year there was no winter," Alix moans. "After the

curse, the weather was sunny and beautiful all year. How were we supposed to know that wouldn't last?"

My mother turns to Alix, her expression morphing immediately from one of stress to sympathy. "Don't worry, I'll fix it."

"You'll fix the weather?" I ask dubiously.

"Yes! Well, no, Aurelia will. Don't even worry about it for another moment, I'll take care of it."

I grimace. Aurelia has a lot of magic, but changing the weather is a nearly impossible task. She tried it once before, and Fox was insistent she stop. He never gets worked up about anything, so we all took that seriously. I'm tempted to remind my mother of that fact, but Alix looks so relieved that I keep my mouth shut.

"What's wrong with the cake?" I ask, turning to the baker.

The woman wrings her hands. "I'm so sorry, Your Majesty! I was working on the cake at home. I ran out of sugar and left for a few hours to get more in the village, then came back to find the cake destroyed."

"Destroyed how?" Alix asks.

"Someone threw a rock through my window and smashed it. The cake was knocked onto the floor. I'm so sorry."

"Can't you make another one?" I ask. "There's still a few days until the wedding."

The baker looks embarrassed. "I can, but the ingredients were all so expensive. I can't afford to replace everything myself."

I wave her off. "Money isn't important. We'll pay for another cake if you can bake it in time. Mother, can you—"

"Yes, of course," my mother trills. She reaches for the baker's arm and pulls her back toward the kitchen. "Come along, I'll find you the money so you can get started right away."

"Someone threw a rock through the baker's window to destroy our cake?" Alix echoes the moment the baker has left. "Who would do that?"

I put a hand on her back. "Don't worry about it, Peaches. Come on, we have one more wish to grant."

We turn back to the throne room and push the doors open. Inside, standing in the center aisle with the golden thrones towering over them, are two men. One is a stooped, elderly Fae man with graying hair. The other one is a pain in my ass.

"Connell!" I snap, my voice echoing around the room. "What are you doing here?"

The elderly man jumps at the sound of my voice, but Connell only turns toward us and grins. "Morning!" he says brightly.

It's not morning—at best, it's mid-afternoon, but that's just Connell. I'm not sure he knows what color the sky is half the time.

Somewhere between houseguest and prisoner, Connell's existence is only one of the many problems to come out of Odessa and Kastian's trip to Hydratta earlier this year—the other problems being that there is now a new queen of questionable morals running our closest neighboring country, and both my best friend and my sister are magically bound to spend six months out of every year on their cursed ship.

The former captain of *The Sea Witch*, James Connell, is human. At least, he was.

Since coming to live here, we've learned that he was born in Alix's world somewhere in the late 1800s. He was twenty-three when he accidentally found his way into Ellender, stowed away aboard a British merchant ship that was lost in a storm and subsequently became the captain of the ship that Kastian and Odessa are now bound to.

After turning over his captaincy to Kastian, Connell lost his immortality—or so we think. Since the curse that once affected him has been transferred to Kastian, we need to understand as much about it as possible. Connell is living here in Vernallis, both because he has nowhere else to go, and because we've decided it's best to keep an eye on him to see if he starts aging or shows any other signs that the curse affected him.

"I was just entertaining your guest," Connell says brightly. "Poor hospitality to leave him waiting so long, don't you think? Not very royal of you."

Beside me, Kastian grinds his teeth. "Where's Jett?"

Connell shrugs. "Don't know. Don't care. You can't expect me to always know where our wayward assassin is at any given moment."

The old man stiffens at the word "assassin" and his eyes widen as he takes a step back from Connell. I shake my head, sighing wearily. Jett isn't an assassin—usually—but that doesn't feel like a point worth making at the moment. "Actually, no. We don't expect you to know where he is; *he* should know where *you* are."

Connell is supposed to be Jett's problem—after all, he was the one who brought the man here in the first place. It's a bit like Jett brought home a stray puppy and that puppy turned out to be a wolf. He's Jett's problem now, and if he bites anyone, Jett will be the one responsible.

Kas steps forward. "Right. Come with me. We're going to go find Jett."

Connell sighs theatrically. "Right-o. You can't blame a man for trying to meet some new people; all of you are so miserably boring."

I scowl as Kastian leads Connell out of the room and shuts

the door behind him, leaving Alix and me alone with the elderly man. I turn to face him. "Our apologies for that."

The man shakes his head vigorously. "No, not at all, your majesties," he breathes, bowing. "My name is Nikolas. Thank you for meeting with me."

I want to point out that we don't exactly have a choice, but I hold it together. Instead, I ask: "What can we do for you?"

The man's face crumples with anguish, making the wrinkles on his old face all the more pronounced. He must be very old indeed to look like that. Fae do age eventually, but it takes centuries. Nikolas must be well over a thousand, and therefore shouldn't be underestimated no matter how weak he looks. Still, there's a moment where I think Nikolas might actually collapse, so I gesture at the nearest chair—which happens to be my throne. He doesn't sit. Instead, he clasps his hands together in front of his chest like someone about to pray or beg.

"I wouldn't be here if I had any other options," he whispers, and even the acoustics of our domed, half-constructed ceiling can't bounce his words loud enough to make them seem less desperate. "I need help."

I try to keep my face expressionless, but Alix immediately softens. She shifts her weight onto one leg and cocks her head. "With what?"

"My grandchildren are missing," Nikolas says, looking down at his boots.

I wait, but he doesn't elaborate, so I clear my throat. "When did you last see them?"

He blinks, as if surprised by the question's simplicity. "Yesterday, just after supper. They'd finished their lessons and were playing in the alley behind my shop. I closed early, like I always do, to walk them home, but when I came out, they were gone." His voice cracks on the word "gone."

"Did you check with their friends? Sometimes kids run off —" Alix starts.

"They would not run," Nikolas insists, voice rising. "They wouldn't have anywhere to go. Their parents died two years ago, and I'm the only family they have left."

"If they disappeared last night, why are you just coming to see us now?" I ask, glancing at the sky outside the nearest stained-glass window. It's midafternoon. If he's being truthful, the children have been missing now for close to 24 hours.

Nikolas swallows thickly. "I went to the local guards first. They helped look, but we didn't find anything. Finally, one of your soldiers sent me to speak with his commander."

"Fox?" I ask. He's the only commander we have, aside from me.

Nikolas nods. "Yes. He told me to come see you directly."

I frown slightly. Fox is one of my four closest friends in the world, but he's not exactly a warm man. I wouldn't have expected him to take pity on this old man to the point of sending him to Alix and me. I'll have to ask him about it.

"What are the children's names?" Alix asks.

"Archer and Gwen," he answers. "Archer is twelve and Gwen is eight." His gaze flicks between us, equal parts hope and terror. "Please. You have to help me find them."

Alix reaches out and puts a hand on Nikolas's shoulder. "We'll look into it," she says, and I swear the man's knees buckle a little as he sighs in relief. "Aside from you, who was the last person who might have seen them?"

He thinks about it for a moment. "Their teacher, I suppose. They attend school at the new schoolhouse in the center of the village. Their teacher's name is Madam Merriweather."

"Alight. Just give us one moment; we'll be right back." I jerk my head to the side for Alix to follow me.

She gives Nikolas another pat on the shoulder, then follows me toward the only patch of privacy the "throne room" has to offer—a half-finished alcove behind a crooked tapestry.

"I know what you're going to say," Alix whispers, beating me to it. "We don't have time for this."

I shake my head. "That's not what I was going to say. Of course we have to help him, both because it's an official request during the wishing time and because I'm not going to ignore two missing kids."

She smiles slightly. "Oh. Okay, good. Then what's wrong?"

"I was going to ask if we can get out of visiting your mother. We don't have long until the wedding, and the longer those kids are missing, the more likely it is they're going to get hurt. We can't waste time traveling to the human realm."

Alix scowls. "Fuck, I keep forgetting. I swear to God, I'm subconsciously blocking out this trip."

"So we don't have to go?"

She gnaws on her lip. "No...we do. Or, I do, at least. It's not just about visiting my mother for Christmas, I'm also going to bring my nana back here with me for the wedding, and she can't travel through the portal without me."

She reaches up and runs her fingers over the necklace that both keeps her from aging and gives her enough of a magical signature to open portals between worlds any time she wants. It's the only good thing my brother ever invented.

"We can't *not* help." Her eyes flick up to mine, dark and urgent. "But also, I don't want to disappoint my mom. She's already suspicious that you don't exist, I don't know how much longer I can get away with her believing I live in 'Ireland.'" She makes quotes with her fingers.

The thought hangs over us: we'll either be the kind of rulers who let kids vanish on their watch, or the kind of daughter who ditches her own mother for a political crisis. Is there a third option?

"Maybe we can do both?" I say, not believing it even as I say it.

She gives me a look that is somehow affectionate and exasperated at the same time and shakes her head. "No, the only thing to do is for me to go visit my mother and you stay here and find the kids. It's not perfect and my mom will definitely think I made you up, but..." she trails off and shrugs.

I grimace. She's right, but this also means that we'll be losing even more time together over the next day or so. At this rate, the next time I'm going to see her is when we're saying our vows.

"Focus on the honeymoon," Alix says, seeming to read my mind. "Just two more days."

I groan. Two days has never felt so long.

## ALIX

My head bursts through the surface of the lake, and I gasp for air.

Before I've even blinked the pond scum from my eyes, a car horn honks twice and I look up, spotting a familiar red sports car.

"Ali!" Nana shouts through her open window. "There are towels and fresh clothes in the back seat. Change fast so I can hug you."

Nana is the only one who has ever called me Ali, and hearing it is nostalgic. I grin and wade through the water toward her.

Portals between Ellender and the human world aren't always in water, but the most convenient portal for me happens to be in the pond in our backyard. It comes out in a small lake off the side of a highway in upstate New York, and unfortunately that means I'm always soaking wet when I pass between worlds.

At least the pond isn't frozen, I'd been slightly worried about that. The portal behind our house in Vernallis never freezes no matter how cold the ground is around it, but I wasn't sure that would be true in the human realm. Evidently it is, but even though there's no ice, it's still December in New York and the air is cold as fuck.

I reach Nana's car and open the rear passenger door. My cheeks ache from smiling and from the cold as I fumble with the buttons of my soaked shirt, peeling it off and reaching for the dry cotton T-shirt Nana packed for me. The fabric catches on my damp skin.

"I should see if I can buy the land this pond is on," I mutter as I twist awkwardly in the cramped backseat, banging my elbow against the window with a dull thud. "I'd put a house here, so I'd have somewhere better to change."

"That's a good point," Nana says thoughtfully. "Let me see what I can do about that."

I grin because I know she's serious. Nana is one of the most famous authors alive today, but it's only in the last few years that she's lived like it. For decades she was stuck emotionally in her past and never spent a cent of her enormous fortune.

Now, since I discovered Ellender and Nana was able to talk about her experiences with someone who knew she wasn't crazy, she's finally started living again. She's been traveling a lot —mostly in the human realm, but occasionally back and forth to Ellender. She finally sold her dangerous old house in Ironhill back to the government and bought a beautiful Victorian mansion in upstate New York. She claims that she likes the privacy of living in the middle of nowhere, but I know that the proximity to the portal is most of the draw of this area.

Once dressed, I climb out of the backseat and walk around the car to the driver's side. Nana opens her door and gets out to hug me. "I've missed you, Ali-girl."

"Me too," I say thickly. After a long second I pull away. "Did you bring my phone?"

"It's in the glove compartment."

"Thank god, I'm going through withdrawal."

She laughs as we both get back in the car. "You would think real magic would be a substitute for your iPhone."

"You would think," I agree, "But no, I miss it. I need my dopamine fix."

Nana chuckles lightly and turns on the radio before backing her car away from the lake and turning toward the little dirt road that leads to the busy highway.

I reach into the glove compartment and fish out my phone and press the power button. The screen flickers to life with a soft blue glow. For a second, I'm excited, but immediately a dozen texts start to come in one after another. Every single one of them is from my mom. I sigh. "And it's ruined."

I've been living in a literal other world for two years now, and my mother still has no clue. Nana and I agreed that telling her wouldn't be a good idea. She would never wait long enough for us to prove it before she tried to have us committed to padded cells...all in the name of our own well-being, of course.

Now, I have to travel back and forth through the portal every week or so because my mother believes that I'm living in Ireland with bad cell service and can only talk when I leave my house to go grocery shopping. She knows Daemon exists, but she thinks he's a reclusive billionaire who hates technology and lives in an old Irish castle. I might have stolen the idea straight out of one of my favorite romance novels...and really, it's not that far from the truth.

At least I was able to make a relatively clean break from the human world, and my mother is my only real loose end. When Daemon first found me, my marriage was ending, I had no friends and no job. There was no one except my mom and Nana to notice or care when I disappeared. Therefore my transition from broke musician to Fae queen was actually much more seamless than it would have been for most people.

I guess it could be worse.

"So," I sigh, settling back into my seat as we drive down the highway. "What have I missed?"

"Nothing interesting," Nana says dismissively. "The world is on fire as usual."

"Mom seems chatty," I comment, holding up my phone for Nana to see the many texts. "Did something happen?"

"Your mother is in a bad mood."

"What else is new?"

She smiles. "More so than usual, I mean. Kevin's daughter from his first marriage is staying with them for Christmas and she's driving your mother crazy. The only thing she's been happy about was you and Daemon visiting...speaking of which, where is he?"

I sigh. "He couldn't come. There's still a lot of wedding planning to do, and some children went missing from the village."

Nana sighs. "We'd better start thinking of an excuse, your mother isn't going to be happy that you've avoided letting her meet him...again."

"I'm not avoiding it," I lie. Nana shoots me a disbelieving look and I grimace. "Okay, I'm avoiding it a little. Mom is already suspicious about my spontaneous move to 'Ireland.'

I'm afraid she'll grill Daemon and he won't be able to answer her normal human questions. I've been preparing him, but do you have any idea how hard it is to explain basic shit like airports to an immortal Fae man whose only meaningful experience in the human world was during World War I?"

Nana reaches over and pats my leg. "Well, you've got a few hours to think of an excuse. It'll take that long to drive back to Philadelphia."

"I've been starting to think we should tell her," I say.

Nana grimaces. "Well, I'm glad you think so because honestly I'm not sure how much longer you'll have a choice. Unless you want to fake your death, I suppose."

I laugh, but Nana doesn't join in.

She's not joking.

Nana's car rumbles into my mother's neighborhood, which is so aggressively suburban the HOA probably has drones that fire warning shots if your recycling bin tips over.

We coast past rows of perfectly cubed hedges, every house straining under the weight of synchronized Christmas lights. My mother's place is the worst offender—a beige brick monstrosity with an illuminated reindeer army and a ten-foot inflatable Santa so menacing I suspect it comes alive at night. There are even lights on the mailbox. Where did she plug them in?

Nana snorts as we pull into the driveway, making a show of shading her eyes against the blinding decorations. "She's outdone herself this year," she mutters, and I can't tell whether she means it as a compliment or a cry for help.

"I've always thought being a tacky Christmas-lover was one of mom's best traits, actually," I comment, getting out of the car. "I kind of like it. There is no Christmas in Ellender. I mean, there's Yule, but that's a lot less...commercial."

Before we can even ring the bell, the front door opens, and my mother—hair shellacked to perfection and heels sky-high—waves us inside while simultaneously shouting instructions at someone on speakerphone. "No, Kevin, I don't care what the pilot said, you don't just sit around an airport bar for eight hours, you get on the next plane."

"I don't know what you want me to do, Iris," Kevin replies patiently, his voice blaring out of the speakerphone. "There is no next plane. There's a blizzard out here. No planes are leaving the airport for at least the next 24 hours."

"So rent a car, or bribe someone, I don't know!" She glares at her phone like it personally invented winter weather. "It's Christmas!"

Nana does this little cough I know is supposed to be a greeting. I try to wedge myself between the nearest mountain of gift bags and a cluster of poinsettias so I can get my "hello" in, but Mom's focus is laser-trained on her phone.

There's a sudden crash upstairs, followed by a plaintive shriek. My mother's eyes twitch but she doesn't pause her rant. "Excuse me," she says, and smacks the mute button. "Ruby, if that was the sound of my Christmas village tipping over, you'll be doing the dishes by hand for the rest of your natural life!" she bellows upward, then unmutes. "No, not you, Kevin, I was talking to the child." A pause. "YOUR child," she adds, pointedly.

I snake around to the staircase, my socks slipping on the

polished wood, and peer up at the landing. Ruby—my college-aged step-sister—stands clutching a white rabbit the size of a small dog. She's petite and blonde, and wearing a black mini dress, sharp black eyeliner and red-and-black striped tights. Her rabbit is wearing a matching striped sweater. She's cooler at nineteen than I ever was, and I'm honestly a tiny bit afraid of her.

"Hey," I say casually.

Ruby lifts her chin. "Hey. Where's the billionaire?"

"Not here," I sigh.

She gives me a look, then shrugs. "That sucks."

*It does. It does suck.*

"Heard you're eloping," Ruby says. "Badass. Iris has been rage-Googling wedding venues all afternoon."

I almost laugh but it comes out as a nervous hiccup. "Wedding venues?"

"Yeah. Get ready, she wants to ambush you into having the wedding here while you're visiting...but since your guy isn't here, I guess that's out. Good luck."

"I should have stayed home," I groan, more to myself than to Ruby.

She answers anyway. "Yeah, probably. I wouldn't be here either but my entire dorm closed for the holidays. That should be illegal, like, people *live* there. Whatever. I'll be down in a second, I just need to put Thackeray away." She smirks and vanishes into my childhood bedroom, which she seems to have taken over. I wonder vaguely where I'm supposed to sleep tonight, but don't care enough to worry much about it.

Back in the kitchen, Nana is already pouring herself a mug of something suspiciously dark—it might be coffee, but more likely it's mostly whiskey. My mother, having finally hung up, rounds on me with a sigh so melodramatic it's giving telenovela.

"Alixandrea," she says, stretching my name to three distinct syllables. "You're late. And wet. And you didn't bring Daemon."

"I'm not wet," I argue gloomily. I'm not—at least not anymore. My hair totally dried in the car. Mostly.

I expect a hug or at least a perfunctory pat on the arm, but instead she circles me like a bomb-sniffing dog. I brace for impact.

"I texted you," she says, brandishing her phone as evidence. "Several times. Some of us plan ahead, you know."

"I know," I say, but she steamrolls right over it.

"I rearranged the entire weekend thinking he'd be here. I even set an extra place at the table. You could have told me sooner if he wasn't coming."

I wring my hands. "Sorry. Complications with the wedding, and he's got responsibilities at home, so..."

Mom's eyes narrow. "Well, if he doesn't get his priorities straight now, he never will." She turns on her heel and marches toward the dining room.

Nana catches my eye and holds out her mug. "Want some?"

I shake my head. "Not yet. I need to be sober for this interrogation."

Nana shrugs. "More for me, then."

We both trail after my mother into the living room.

"Where's Kevin?" I ask, trying to take the focus off me. "Did I hear him say there's a blizzard?"

My mom scowls. "He had a business trip last week, but the weather has been so bad he's still stuck in Boston. I told him he should have driven."

"I'm sorry," I say honestly. "So he won't be home for Christmas?"

Her lips tighten into a thin line. "No. So, I guess we'll both be single this week."

"Mmm," I give her a noncommittal hum. It doesn't feel like the best moment to tell her I'm not staying all week, just tonight...and maybe not even that long.

The rest of the afternoon passes by almost normally. After her initial disappointment that Daemon isn't here my mother calmed down. Even so, dinner is a stilted affair. The table is set for six, even though there are only four of us, and Mom keeps glancing at the empty chairs and scowling.

She interrogates me about the wedding—dates, colors, whether Daemon's family has "noble blood"—and every answer I give seems to offend her more. Nana attempts to deflect, but Mom's resolve is ironclad. Ruby and the rabbit—which my mother doesn't even seem to notice is sitting in Kevin's empty chair—eat silently, occasionally exchanging glances like they're plotting a prison break.

After dessert, Mom follows me into the living room and lowers herself dramatically onto the couch, patting the cushion next to her. I sit. She takes my hand in hers. "Alixandrea," she says, "I am your mother."

"Oh, I am well aware, Mom." *It's not like I had any choice in the matter.*

"Are you? I'm not sure."

I sigh and pull my hands from her grip. "What do you mean?"

"You are eloping. Fine. It's not my preference, but you're an adult."

"Am I? Because this conversation feels like you think I'm still fifteen."

"I know you're a grown woman, but it's still my right—no, my duty—as your mother to ensure your wedding is not a disaster. You didn't even ask if you could wear my dress."

I blink. "Mom, we don't exactly have the same style. It honestly didn't occur to me to ask. Are we even the same size?"

"We could have it altered to fit you. I'm sure they could let it out in the waist."

I roll my eyes so hard I'm surprised they don't stick. "Which dress do you mean? The one you wore to marry dad or to marry Kevin?"

"Your father, obviously." Her tone is wounded. "God, Alixandrea, the way you talk to me you'd think I was a monster."

I take a deep breath, readying for the annual family martyrdom parade. "You're not a monster, Mom. You're just..." I reach for a finish line that isn't a land mine.

She waits, lips pursed in undisguised anticipation.

"...really enthusiastic about holidays," I offer. "I didn't think you'd want to worry about the wedding since it's Christmastime."

The corners of her mouth twitch upward, the tiniest hint of a smile. "Well, it's a mother's job to care. So. That's settled. You'll wear the dress so at least I have photos I can display."

I blink. "Wait what? Which dress?"

"The dress," she hisses, enunciating every letter like it's a threat. "My dress."

"Um, no. I'm sorry, but I already have a dress."

She glares. "You already picked a dress. Without me."

Oh god, here we go. "Do you remember dress shopping for my first wedding? Did you really think that was a good time?"

She scoffs. "It was a cherished memory."

"It was traumatizing. It gave me flashbacks to bathing suit shopping in middle school."

"You're exaggerating."

"I'm not. Anyway, I had the dress made in Ireland, I couldn't just invite you to come along."

She locks eyes with me, and it's clear that she is assembling her arsenal of motherly guilt for a siege. "Well, let me see it at least."

"I didn't bring it," I say quickly.

She rolls her eyes. "Obviously. Show me a picture."

"I don't have a picture. My camera's broken." She frowns at me, and I can feel the lie crumbling. I scramble for something, anything, to throw on the pile. "And also, it's bad luck," I add helplessly.

"That's for the groom, not the mother," she snaps.

I glance at Nana for backup, but Nana is suddenly fascinated by the twinkling Christmas lights outside the window and refuses to meet my eyes.

My mother's eyes narrow. "You know, sometimes I wonder if you're even telling us the truth."

My stomach lurches. "About what?"

She waves a manicured hand. "All of this! Ireland, the man, your future. You barely call, you barely text. Sometimes you disappear for weeks at a time. It's not normal, Alixandrea."

"I'm just busy," I say lamely. "And we have almost no cell service, I keep telling you that."

Mom presses on, relentless. "And this man, this Daemon. I've never met him. He doesn't have social media. He doesn't even have a LinkedIn! Who doesn't have a LinkedIn in this century?"

I snort, picturing Daemon using LinkedIn, then instantly regret it when my mother's expression turns even icier.

She pounces. "See, you don't even take it seriously! What's going on with you? Is it drugs?"

I feel a headache blooming just behind my left eye. "Do I look like I'm on drugs to you?"

She stands up, angrily pacing around the room. "How should I know? You're getting married to a man none of us have met, in a country none of us have visited. I just want to meet him, Alixandrea. I want to see the life you've made."

For a second, I feel a pang of guilt. Then I remember: if I invite my mother to my "life," she will discover that my fiancé is not human and that my immediate circle of friends includes a bunch of escaped Fae convicts and one actual siren.

"I promise, you'll meet him soon. What if we come back to visit in January?"

"That's not good enough," she says, voice trembling with the force of her own sense of injustice.

"I'm sorry? What does that mean?"

Nana finally intervenes. "Iris, give the girl a break. She's had a long trip. Let's just enjoy the evening, shall we?"

Mom sits up straighter, her hands balling into fists. "If you won't explain what's going on or bring your fiancé here to meet me, then I'll just have to go to you."

I splutter, choking on air. "Excuse me? Come to us where?"

"In Ireland. Isn't that where you live? What town, I'm not sure you've ever told me."

I look frantically over at Nana, who sits up straighter. "When would you have time to visit, Iris? Calm down."

"I have time right now," she says, reaching into her pocket

for her phone. "When is your return flight Alixandrea? I'll see if there are still seats left."

"Wait, no!"

She narrows her eyes dangerously at me. "Why not?"

*Fuck, fuck, fuck!*

I look at Nana, who just shrugs. "Should have faked your death," she mutters.

My mom rounds on Nana. "What was that? Do you know what's going on here?"

I pinch the skin on the bridge of my nose and close my eyes. "Okay, mom, fine. You win. There's something I need to tell you."

Mom's face splits into a smug grin and she puts her phone back in her pocket before settling back on the couch. "I'm all ears."

DAEMON

I fucking hate snow.

Even as a kid I never liked the cold, but after wasting two-thirds of my life freezing my ass off in Dyaspora, I've developed a special kind of loathing for it.

Today, though, the snow doesn't look quite as bad as usual. The road to the village is picturesque, the snow falling in fat flakes. Red ribbons flutter from the lampposts, and someone has wound pine garlands around the trunks of the oak trees. When we reach the high street, the decorations are even more excessive. Candle flames dance in every window, baubles hang from rafters and a burst of laughter and the chorus of an old drinking song spill from the pub's open door as a man stumbles out, his cheeks flushed with ale and firelight.

In contrast, my friends and I are silent and stoic as we walk.

They don't typically like snow either, but I know that's not the problem. Fox, Jett, and Kastian decided to tag along on my search for Nikolas's missing grandchildren, and the seriousness of the situation is affecting all of us. Even Jett, who is always smiling, scowls darkly.

He doesn't say it, but I know what he's thinking. Nobody wants to be the one to find out the missing kids are actually... well, missing.

Ellender is a dangerous place, and sometimes people disappear. Jett was one of those kids who ended up living on the street with a pack of other orphans and runaways. He's never told us exactly how he ended up there, but I wonder if this situation hits too close to home.

"Where are we even supposed to start?" Jett asks, cutting into my thoughts. "Do we just go door to door? Or search the woods?"

"Kids don't just vanish," Kastian cuts in. "They always have a reason to run, or a place they like to hide. If we find out where that is, we'll find them."

"I don't know where to start," I admit. "I'm hoping it will help to talk to their teacher. Maybe she knows where they typically go to play."

Fox reaches up and dusts snow from his blonde hair. "It's cold," he says, stating the obvious.

I throw him a sideways look. If it were Jett making such an obvious statement, I'd tell him to shut up and use his brain, but with Fox I'm inclined to take him more seriously.

Fox isn't much of a talker, but after knowing him for decades I know that his lack of talking isn't because he has nothing to say. He's probably the smartest of all of us, and doesn't explain himself because he thinks whatever has already occurred to him should be obvious to everyone else. Like, when I asked why he'd sent Nikolas to talk to me, he just said: "They're kids," and left it at that.

"What's your point?" I ask.

He looks sour, like he always does when he has to explain himself. "They disappeared last night, and it was cold then too. If they're still alive, then they would have taken shelter somewhere. We should be looking for them in caves or abandoned houses, not in their schoolyard."

I cock my head. "Fair enough, but I still want to talk to the teacher and maybe some of the other children."

He shrugs. "As long as it doesn't take too long. It'll be dark soon."

I nod grimly, and put my head down as we all walk a bit faster toward the school.

We find the teacher in the school courtyard, where children in half-finished pine cone crowns and garlands of mistletoe and ivy shuffle through some kind of synchronized dance.

As we draw closer, I notice how dejected the children look. A boy drops his ribbon wand. A girl's eyes well with tears as she stares at two empty spots in their formation.

The teacher claps her hands twice to get the children's attention, then freezes mid-motion when she spots us at the gate. Her smile stretches too wide as she smooths her apron and curtsies so quickly she nearly loses her balance. "Your Majesty!"

The children pivot toward us, their faces droopy and sad. I

lift my hand in greeting. The teacher's voice rises an octave. "Everyone rest for a moment," she calls, then adds with sudden sharpness, "Stay where I can see you."

"Afternoon," I greet her, closing the space between us. "Are you Madam Merriweather?"

"Yes!" the woman gushes. "Are you here about the children's procession? I wouldn't have expected you to come personally, but I'm sure they would be happy to show you what we're working on."

"The children's procession?" I echo, confused.

"For the wedding," she clarifies.

It takes me a long moment to understand what the fuck she's talking about, then I vaguely recall a conversation between Alix and my mother about the local school children from the village helping to carry the train of Alix's dress. I didn't realize that would require so much rehearsal.

"No, actually. We're here about two missing children."

The teacher's face falls. "Oh. Of course, I should have realized. Would you all like to step away with me for a moment? The children are traumatized enough as is by the disappearance of their friends. I'm trying to stay upbeat because I don't want to upset them further."

As if on cue, a small girl with blonde braids tugs at the teacher's skirt. Her bottom lip trembles as she whispers, just loud enough for us to hear, "Did the witch take Gwen and Archer?"

The teacher's face tightens. She crouches down, smoothing the child's hair with a practiced gentleness. "No, Lily. There's no witch. Remember what we talked about?" The girl nods, but looks unconvinced, her eyes darting toward the edge of the woods beyond the courtyard.

The teacher jerks her head toward the hallway and we all follow her outside.

"See?" she asks. "They're all convinced that Archer and Gwen were taken by the Yule witch and nothing I say can convince them otherwise."

I grimace. I hadn't given a second of thought to the Yule witch—it's just a legend meant to discourage kids from wandering off. Even when I was a child myself, I never believed it. But, then again, no one I knew ever disappeared like Archer and Gwen.

"Can you tell us about the children?" I ask.

Madam Merriweather sighs and runs a hand through her hair. "They're both such wonderful students. Gwen is eight. She's very bright and enjoys reading. Archer is twelve. He's been a bit of a handful this year, but overall a good boy."

"A handful in what way?"

She shrugs. "He's old enough that his magic is a little unpredictable, but it's not his fault. He's never meant to break anything or cause trouble."

Madam Merriweather points toward a window that I only now notice is broken. "He did that just last week, I haven't gotten around to fixing it yet. Whenever he gets startled or angry, things break but he's hardly the first twelve-year-old boy I've taught to have that problem, he'll grow out of it."

We all nod in general understanding. I vividly remember how at the same age I couldn't get a handle on my magic either. I once tried to turn on a lamppost and it exploded.

Without thinking, I raise a hand toward the window and the glass immediately knits itself back together. The teacher offers me a genuine smile. "Thank you."

"So both the kids have magic, then?" Kastian asks. "Do

most of the village children practice magic or are they unusual?"

"I wouldn't say it's unusual, but they're certainly in the minority. Of course you know that magic must be trained from a very early age to be of any use, and most village children don't have access to that sort of tutoring."

"You don't teach them?" I ask.

She shakes her head. "I don't use magic either. I never had the opportunity to learn."

"Then who taught Archer and Gwen?"

"They were both trained from an early age by their parents. Since the parents died, they have fallen behind a bit, but they're both naturally gifted."

"Can you think of any reason the children would have run away?" Kastian asks.

The teacher shakes her head. "No."

"We were told they're orphans," Jett supplies.

The teacher nods. "Yes, but they were both relatively well-adjusted to the death of their parents a few years ago. I was happy that they were doing so well living with their grandfather."

"How did the parents die?" Jett presses, eyes widening slightly.

"During the curse," Madam Merriweather says sadly. "Lots of people died then, it wasn't exactly unexpected."

I nod in understanding. "Do you know if they like living with their grandfather?"

"Yes, as far as I know."

I frown. The teacher seems to be a nice woman, but she's not being very helpful. "What do you think happened?" I probe.

She shakes her head. "I don't know. I'm too old to believe

in the witch, but I am afraid they got dragged off by a wolf or something. I'm so worried about them."

"Maybe they're lost in the woods," a small voice pipes up.

We turn and see the same little girl with blonde pigtails leaning out of the door to the classroom. Clearly, she's been listening.

I bend down to her eye level, then stall. I've never spent much time around kids and I don't know how to talk to them. "Hi. I'm Daemon," I say, after a second.

Behind me the teacher splutters. "That's the king, Lily. You call him 'Your Majesty.'"

"Don't worry about that," I tell Lily.

Lily looks between us with wide questioning eyes as the teacher squawks in protest. I run a hand through my hair nervously. I'm probably confusing the poor kid.

I change tactics. "What's your name?" I ask her, even though I've heard the teacher use it several times now.

"Lily," she answers shyly.

"Were you friends with Gwen?"

She shakes her head. "She's older than me. She's friends with my sister."

I'm tempted to ask to speak to the sister instead, but Lily seems chatty and alert for such a young child. It's probably worth seeing what else she knows. "Did you see anything happen to Gwen or her brother?"

Again, Lily shakes her head. "I didn't see anything, but all the older kids like to play in the woods. It's a game about who's brave enough to go the furthest away from the others during witch season."

My stomach sinks. If they've been in the woods all night, then the likelihood of them being attacked by an animal or otherwise hurt just went up tenfold. "Were they playing that game yesterday?"

She nods. I smile at her, even as her teacher's voice rises behind me. "The woods are forbidden. You should all know better."

I tune out the sounds of Madam Merriweather scolding Lily and get to my feet again. I catch Kastian's eye and he tilts his head slightly toward the tree line, one eyebrow raised.

"Come on," I mutter. "The sooner we start combing the woods the better chance we have of finding them."

I don't say the part we're all thinking—we might still find them, but whether they'll be alive when we do is becoming less and less likely by the minute.

## ALIX

For the second time in less than a day, I burst out of the center of a freezing pond.

Instantly, a high-pitched wail of terror reaches me. I flail in the water, looking around frantically for my mom. She too has emerged from the pond, her mouth wide and eyes bulging. Her designer jacket is plastered to her windmilling arms, sending water droplets flying like tiny crystals in the winter air.

"How dare you!" she shrieks "What the—"

"Mom, calm down!" I yell, splashing toward her.

"*Calm down,* Alixandrea? *Really*? Is this some kind of sick joke to you?"

*Oh, if only it were.*

I realized the moment my mom insisted on visiting "Ireland" that I was caught. I had to tell her the truth. Except, you can never tell my mother anything. I had to show her, and the only way to do it was to drag her kicking and screaming into the portal lake—literally. We left Ruby at home alone—she was only too happy to be rid of my mother—and made the long drive back to the portal.

Only now, I'm second guessing everything.

Nana's head pops out of the water next to me and looks over at my mom, who is muttering angrily under her breath. "I hope you know what you're doing, Ali-girl."

I sigh. *So do I.*

My mom claws her way toward the bank, her soaked sweater clinging to her shoulders, teeth chattering so hard I can hear them from here. I don't think she's yet realized that we're not in the same lake that I pushed her into mere moments ago, or that it wasn't snowing in New York.

"Wait, Mom—" I swim after her, but it's too late to stop her.

Summoned by all the noise, Aurelia, Odessa, and Beatrix come running out of the house. Pausing at the edge of the water, mom looks up at the sound of their footsteps and I can see the exact moment she realizes that the enormous mansion and sprawling rose garden were definitely not there a second ago. Then, she focuses on the three women running toward us and her eyes bug out of her head.

Odessa glides forward, one pale hand extended toward my mother. "Let me help you."

Mom scrambles backward in the mud, crab-like. Her voice cracks. "Stay back!"

I sigh. I feel a little guilty. I mean, I'd feel guiltier if my mom hadn't backed me into this corner in the first place, but still...I'd forgotten how frightening the Fae seemed to me when

I first arrived, and especially Odessa, who is so beautiful that my brain immediately registered her existence as *wrong*.

"Mom, it's okay—" I begin, but never get to finish.

"Here, let me fix that!" Obviously trying to help, Aurelia holds out both hands. Golden light spirals from her fingertips toward my mom's drenched jacket, and steam rises from the fabric.

My mom's gaze drops to her suddenly dry clothes, then back to Aurelia's glowing hands, then over to me. There's a combination of betrayal and fear in her face before her eyes roll back into her head.

"Catch her!" I yell, but it wasn't necessary. Odessa is already reaching instinctively for my mom, grabbing her by the shoulders before she crumples into the water.

I look helplessly around at everyone and shrug. "I guess it could have been worse."

It's early evening by the time my mother calms down, and snow is pelting the darkened windows.

Odessa, Beatrix and Aurelia sit on one side of the long kitchen table, steam unfurling from the mugs of tea in front of them. On the opposite side of the table I sit between my mother and Nana. Mom taps her long nails against the side of her empty mug in an anxious, staccato rhythm.

"Here, take mine," Beatrix says kindly, sliding her own untouched mug of tea toward my mother.

Mom doesn't thank her, but wraps her fingers around the

new mug without drinking. Her knuckles are bright white and she keeps shooting sideways glances at Dessa, like she's going to launch herself across the table and attack us.

I catch Dessa's eye and grimace apologetically. She just shrugs, as if to say, "It happens."

I want to tell my mother that she'll get used to everyone's other-worldly beauty, even Odessa's, but I haven't been able to get a word in for a while.

Nana is leaning over me talking to my mom. Her voice has gone hoarse in the time she's been talking, relaying the entire story of how she first fell into Ellender, escaped, and later wrote her bestselling book about it. We haven't even gotten to the part where I enter the story yet, and I'm not sure we will—at least, not tonight.

Mom stares at Nana as if they're strangers. Her mouth is slightly open, eyes blinking rapidly every few seconds like she's trying to clear her vision. She looks like she's had about enough insane revelations for one day.

Then, suddenly, she comes back to life.

She sits up straighter and clanks her mug against the table with a sharp crack, sloshing the hot liquid everywhere. She swipes a strand of hair behind her ear, her wedding ring catching the light. "Okay," she says, voice steadier than it's been since she arrived. "Okay, that's enough."

I internally groan, and real guilt washes over me. That's it, I've killed my own mother. She's going to drop dead of shock any second.

"Do you want me to take you home?" I ask.

She swivels and fixes me with the same look she gave me at sixteen when I missed curfew. "No! I want to know where your fiancé is."

I blink at her, nonplussed. "That's what you're worried about?"

"If any man is important enough to drag me through—" she gestures vaguely at the window. "—whatever this is, then I need to meet him."

*Okay then.*

In answer, I turn to Beatrix. "When did Daemon leave?"

"Hours ago," she answers promptly. "He refused to take any guards with him, just Fox, Jett and Kastian."

"That doesn't surprise me. Where did they go?"

"The village," Dessa says. "They went to look for the children."

I frown and glance at the dark window. The snow is coming down harder by the second, pelting at the windows. I'm not worried about Daemon or the others—they've survived far worse than a little snow—but I am worried about the missing children.

"Can't you just call him, Alixandrea?" my mother demands.

I ignore that question and instead dig in my pocket for the heavy gold pocket watch that Daemon gave me last Yule—just past seven in the evening. Incidentally, that's earlier than it was in the human realm when we entered the portal to come here, but time never works perfectly between realms.

I've been trying to think back to two years ago when I first arrived in Ellender. What made me finally believe that the world was real? Aside from the enormous wolf and Daemon's wings, I think it was when we first left the palace and I saw the wider Fae world that the truth really started to sink in.

I'm about to suggest we go into the village after them—if only to get out of the house and give my mother something else to focus on—but I don't get the chance.

The door to the back garden swings open with a gust of cold air, and Connell steps in, snowflakes melting in his dark hair. "Evening!"

"Where did you come from?" I demand without thinking.

He grins at me and winks. "Wouldn't you like to know, darling?"

My mom's spine straightens, as she looks from Connell to me, her eyes widening slightly as she takes him in. His flushed cheekbones catch the firelight as he shrugs off his coat, revealing broad shoulders under a simple linen shirt. She sits up straighter. "So, this is Daemon?"

She sounds almost hopeful and I roll my eyes. Connell is objectively handsome, but he's human, and in my eyes can't hold a candle to Daemon.

"No, Mom, that's Connell..." I trail off trying to figure out how to introduce the pirate. He's not exactly a friend. A guest maybe?

Without missing a beat, Connell gives my mother a sweeping bow. "Pleasure to meet you, my lady."

To my absolute shock, my mother giggles like she's fourteen and holds out her hand to him. Rather than shaking it, he kisses the back of it, and she beams.

Dessa catches my eye and we have to look away from each other immediately or we'll burst out laughing.

"Ignore him, Mom," I say in a choked voice. "He's like that with everyone."

"Not everyone, just the beautiful ladies," Connell says, winking again.

"Alixandrea, who is this?" my mom asks, not taking her eyes off Connell.

"I'm their prisoner," he answers, grinning unhelpfully.

My mom's simpering smile slides off her face and her eyes

bug out of her head. She turns to me, her voice returning to its usual disapproving tone. "Alixandrea, what the hell is going on?"

I pinch the bridge of my nose. *I should have faked my death.*

DAEMON

"Have I mentioned that I fucking hate snow?" I grumble, more to myself than my friends.

No one replies, but I know I'm not alone.

Fox, Jett, and Kastian look as miserable as I am, and the silence is tense as we walk through the woods. The crunch of our boots grows increasingly muffled as the wind picks up and the snow thickens on the forest floor. Long shadows stretch between the darkening pines until it grows difficult to see.

The forest that runs alongside Storia is massive. I know it must end somewhere—the border of Thermia is to the north, and if you walked far enough east, you'd eventually hit the desert of Solistine, but I couldn't begin to fucking guess how long that would take.

I try not to think about it, reminding myself that two kids couldn't have gone that far...hopefully.

Still, my stomach knots tighter with each passing hour. We

haven't found a single shred of evidence that Archer or Gwen was ever here and the temperature's dropping fast.

If they were human children, I'd be certain we would never find them alive. A human would have frozen to death by now, but Fae children can't die from cold. They can still fucking feel it, though, and there are so many other ways to die in these woods.

The sound of chewing makes me stop short and turn around. "What the fuck is that?"

Jett freezes with his hand halfway to his mouth, what looks like half a biscuit clutched in his fist. He swallows and holds the biscuit out to me. "What, you want some?"

"No. Where the hell did you get that?"

"Brought it with me." He shrugs as he takes another bite and crumbs tumble to the ground. Glancing back at the snowy ground behind us, he's made quite a trail of crumbs.

I roll my eyes and turn my back on him, grumbling under my breath. "You're going to attract fucking animals dropping food everywhere. We're supposed to be focused on looking for the kids."

"Wolves don't eat bread, asshole," Jett says through another full mouth, "and I can look and eat at the same time."

"I'm more worried about wolves eating the kids," Kastian comments, putting an abrupt end to me and Jett snapping at each other.

"There are no wolves nearby," Fox says flatly.

I look sideways at him. "How could you know that?"

Predictably he doesn't answer, just trudges purposefully onward.

. . .

Another hour passes and the snow only gets worse.

I hold my hand in front of my face and see nothing but a shadow. The trees have vanished, replaced by looming gray shapes that materialize and disappear with each gust of wind. My eyelashes clump with ice, and every breath scrapes my throat raw. It's like being back in Dyaspora.

"We should go back to the manor," Kastian yells.

He can't be more than a few yards to my right, but his voice still gets lost in the wind.

"Not yet!" I yell back.

"How are we supposed to find anything when we can't fucking see?"

Before I can respond, something catches my eye in the distance. I squint through the snow and my heart leaps. There's a tiny spot of light ahead. A fire maybe or a house? "There's something over there! Let's check that out before we go back."

If they answer me I can't hear it, but it doesn't matter. My legs feel like they've turned to stone, but the light is enough to drag me forward.

We stumble out of the trees and into a little clearing. Up a drifted path that's more crater than walkway, is a cottage. The windows are glazed with frost, but the inside glows like a bonfire.

Kastian gets to the porch first and peers through the frosted window. "You think anyone's home?"

As if in answer, the door swings open and I have to raise a hand to shield my eyes from the sudden bright light.

"Who's there?" A quavering female voice calls into the wind.

I jog forward, then stop short in surprise. "Mrs. Hilde?"

The baker I met this morning is standing in the doorway

squinting through the snow at me. Her face splits into a smile of recognition, and before I can explain what we're doing on her porch during a blizzard, she's ushering us inside. "You poor things! You must be freezing out there! Come in!"

She doesn't have to ask us twice. I lead the way, my friends trailing after me, and we crowd into the small cottage. Mrs. Hilde slams the door behind us, cutting off the wind.

It's really too small a room for all of us, and our shoulders brush the walls on either side, barely leaving room to turn without elbowing each other. The ceiling is hung low and Fox, the tallest of the four of us, has to duck to avoid the rafters. At least it's warm. A fire crackles in the stone hearth, logs shifting with soft pops that send sparks dancing upward. The air smells of baked goods, and I breathe a sigh of relief. "Thank you."

"Of course! Sit down by the fire!" Mrs. Hilde fusses.

I smile. "I'm sorry to bother you like this."

She beams at me, flashing white teeth. "It's not a bother, but what are you doing out here in a storm? This isn't about the cake, is it?"

I shake my head and icy droplets go flying around the cramped room. "No, not at all."

I briefly explain that we're looking for two missing children. Mrs. Hilde's face falls. "Oh, I'm so sorry to hear that."

"Did you happen to see anyone come this way?"

"I've been here baking all day. Except for when I came to speak to you, and bought new ingredients in the village, I haven't left my kitchen." She gestures behind her and I notice a wedding cake on the small wooden counter. It's five tiers high, and the icing looks nearly finished.

I clear my throat, wishing Alix were here since I have no idea what the cake is supposed to look like. "Er, that looks excellent."

She smiles tightly. "I only wish you'd seen the first one. I will never forgive the boy who smashed my window."

"Boy?" I ask, my interest piqued. "It couldn't have been one of the children, was it?"

She shakes her head. "Er, no. I wasn't actually here when it happened."

My brow furrows. "Wait, what?"

She laughs lightly. "Sorry, my mistake, I'm just so flustered you're all here. I should have said that I assumed it was a boy who broke my window. Who else would be throwing rocks?"

I frown. "Alright..."

"Would you like some tea or something to eat?" the baker asks quickly. "Surely there's something I can get you."

I glance back at the dark, frosty windows and frown. "Actually, no. We should probably keep looking for the children."

Jett makes a squawk of protest. "What? Are you insane, Ashwater? I thought we were going to get warm."

I grimace. We were, but now I suddenly have the strangest feeling that I don't want to be here.

"I don't think we're going to find them in the dark while it's snowing," Kastian points out. "We can try again in the morning."

"Fine," I growl. "Then we should go back to the manor. Alix might be back by now."

"Please, at least stay long enough to get warm," Mrs. Hilde insists. "And let me make you some supper. You must be starving." As if on cue, Jett's stomach growls loudly. The baker notices and smiles at him in a motherly way. "Just give me one moment. I'll run downstairs to my pantry. I'm sure I can whip something up for you."

She turns, dusting her hands on her apron, and reaches for

a small door I hadn't noticed before. The hinges groan as it swings open, revealing nothing but darkness and the first few wooden steps of a narrow stairwell descending into shadow. Her plump figure disappears through the doorway, the sound of her footsteps fading with each creak of old wood, until only the four of us remain in the suddenly quiet room.

"I don't want to stay here," I say immediately.

"Why?" Kastian asks curiously.

"Just a feeling. Let's go."

Jett groans. "She's a nice old lady. And she's making your wedding cake, Ashwater. You're paranoid."

"I don't like it either," Fox says flatly. Then, to my surprise, he elaborates. "It smells like death in here."

I raise my eyebrows at him. "It smells like cake."

He shakes his head, but being Fox, doesn't say anything else. Still, an uneasy shiver travels up my spine.

At that moment, a loud crash, like splintering wood, rips through the cottage. I jump, and nearly knock my elbow into the wedding cake. Fox's head smacks against a low beam as he startles upright.

In an instant, I'm alert. I cross the cottage in two strides and yank open the door to the cellar. The smell of damp earth invades my nose. "Mrs. Hilde? Are you alright?"

"Of course, Your Majesty!" She yells back, sounding slightly winded. "Don't worry about me, I'll be right—ow!"

Alarm hits me as she yelps in pain. "What happened?"

"Nothing!" she shouts again.

I glance over my shoulder at the others. Kastian looks tense, Fox worried, and even Jett has stopped smiling. Turning back to the stairs, I take a step into the darkness.

Suddenly, Mrs. Hilde appears at the bottom of the stairs again. She's holding a flower sack with one hand and a jar of what looks to be molasses in the other. "Found what I was looking for!" she says cheerfully. "I'm going to make gingerbread."

"What was that sound?" I demand.

"Oh, nothing," she says as she hurries up the stairs toward me.

I'm forced to step out of the doorway to let her pass, but then I peer back into the darkness. "Let me just go make sure everything is alright."

The stairwell is somehow even narrower than it looked, with damp rock walls that squeeze in close enough to brush my shoulders. It smells like wet earth and something faintly sulfurous, like rotten eggs someone tried to cover up with cinnamon.

My hand finds the wall and I inch downward, hyperaware of Kastian close behind me. Fox and Jett are right behind him, so when Mrs. Hilde tries to protest again, her voice is muffled by four large bodies stubbornly squeezing into a space built for one.

"Really, it's nothing," Mrs. Hilde calls down, her voice ricocheting off the stone. "It's dirty down there, you shouldn't—"

"Kas, conjure a light," I mutter, and the words barely leave my mouth before he responds.

The flare of magic is bright and fast. A little flame materializes in his palm, and throws every shadow into sharp relief.

It also immediately reveals that Mrs. Hilde was lying: the stairs, yes, are filthy, but the bottom of the cellar is anything but.

The floor down here is packed hard and smooth, swept clean of dust, and lined with square flagstones, a distinct improvement over the upper staircase. The shelves along the far wall are stacked high with baking supplies—jars of jam, bottles of cordial, mysterious preserves in brown glass jars, and baskets of brightly wrapped candies. There's even a row of smoked sausages hanging from the ceiling, which draws Jett's attention instantly.

My eyes land on the only thing that seems out of place: splintered wood and cornmeal cover a patch of floor near the wall. It looks as if one of the heavy barrels exploded of its own accord.

I stride over to the broken barrel and bend down to pick up a handful of cornmeal. My brow furrows in confusion.

Kastian's hand lands on my shoulder, startling me. "Do you smell that?" he whispers, low enough that it probably shouldn't carry, but the cellar amplifies every sound.

"Yeah," I say, and everyone else nods. The sulfur smell is stronger here, and now there's an edge of rot to it—something not even cinnamon could hide.

I twist to look at Mrs. Hilde, who is halfway down the stairs and clearly trying to herd us back up. She's clutching the jar of molasses, brandishing it like a weapon. "Don't worry about the mess. One of my barrels just cracked, it's nothing to worry about right now. I have everything I need for ginger-bread. I'll have the cookies ready in no time—"

Fox grabs my arm and pulls me to the left, toward a wall stacked with old potato crates. "There's something behind here."

"Excuse me," Mrs. Hilde barks. "Please don't touch that."

I ignore her. "Someone help me move it."

Jett, who was halfway through stealing a sausage, drops it and comes over to help. The two of us grab the edge of the crate and shove. It's heavy with potatoes, but not so heavy that we can't manage it together. The crate slides to the side with a scraping noise that makes my teeth ache, and behind it is—nothing. Just a wall, rough stone mortared badly together. Except—

"There's a seam here," I say, running my fingers along the line where the stones meet. "Like a hidden door."

Mrs. Hilde shrieks, a high, shattered sound. "Don't touch that! It's dangerous!" she yells, but I'm already pressing my shoulder into the seam and testing it with my weight. Fox and Kastian jump in to help, and together we manage to pry open a narrow wedge of space, just enough to see darkness beyond.

The smell hits us full force, a ripe, wet, animal stink that makes my stomach heave. Jett recoils. "What the fuck is that?"

Kastian's flame flares brighter, casting long shadows across the hidden chamber. The light catches first on something white—a femur, then a skull, then dozens more, scattered like fallen leaves across the packed earth floor. "Holy shit."

A muffled whimper draws my eyes to the far corner where two small, blonde figures huddle against the damp stone. Their wrists are raw from rope burns, mouths stretched around filthy gags. When they see us, their eyes widen, and they thrash wildly and try to scream around the cloth in their mouths.

Rage courses through me and I whip around and see Mrs. Hilde darting back up the stairs. "Grab her!"

Fox's boots scrape against stone as he lunges forward, fingers outstretched toward Mrs. Hilde's apron. The fabric slips through his grasp like water. She scrambles back up the cellar stairs, surprisingly nimble for someone so old. Fox's hand drops to his sword hilt, but it's too late—Mrs. Hilde's silhouette vanishes into the light above and the door slams shut behind her.

DAEMON

Fox and Jett kneel beside the whimpering children, quickly undoing the knots binding their wrists.

Meanwhile, I yank at the cellar door handle as hard as I can, desperate to run after Mrs. Hilde and tear her head from her body. I don't know what the fuck is going on here, and I don't plan to wait to find out. To my fury, however, the door doesn't budge. I raise a hand and try to unlock it with magic, but nothing happens. Frustrated, I slam my shoulder against the wood. "Fuck!"

"Move!" Kastian barks. "Let me try."

I step out of the way and Kas takes my place. He also tries yanking, shoving, and using magic against the door, but nothing works. Finally, he goes so far as to try and light the whole wall on fire, but the flames just bounce off the wood.

We're fucking trapped.

Rage courses through me and I feel myself shaking with the effort of holding it back. How the hell did this happen?

"Ashwater, get down here," Jett calls.

I close my eyes and try to calm down. I need to focus on the kids—that's what really matters here.

I take a few deep breaths and walk back down the stairs into the main room of the cellar. Either Fox or Jett must have replaced the door to the little hidden dungeon, and I'm grateful, as the smell is considerably less potent.

Archer and Gwen are sitting on the floor in the center of the room. They're no longer bound or gagged, but still shaking with fear. Both of them are blonde-haired and bedraggled-looking, but their expressions are different. Archer is eyeing us all suspiciously, while his sister is sobbing and has attached herself to Fox. He's looking somewhat helpless as she clings to his arm.

I suck in a breath, trying to pull myself together for their sake. "Are you two hurt?"

The little girl keeps crying, but the boy answers sharply. "No. Who are you?"

I open my mouth, but Jett beats me to it. "He's the king."

The boy—Archer—eyes me with clear distrust. "Really?"

I have never really been comfortable referring to myself as King anything, even after two years of ruling Vernallis. Now, though, it seems like a good time to show some authority, if only to reassure them that we'll get out of here. I nod. "We've been looking for you."

"Why would a king look for us?" Archer demands.

"Your grandfather sent us to bring you home."

He sneers. "How are you going to do that if you're trapped in here too?"

I can't hold back a small growl of frustration. "We're temporarily trapped. We'll get out of here, don't worry."

He doesn't look convinced and I don't know what to say. I wish Alix were here, I'm *really* not good at talking to kids.

"How did you end up here?" I ask finally.

"The witch captured us!" the girl cries. "She was going to eat us for Yule!"

I grimace. I wish I could tell her that was just a story, but looking around...fuck, maybe it isn't.

"We were out playing in the woods." Archer says. His eyes narrow like he's testing if I'm going to scold him for going into the woods, but I'm not really one to judge.

Archer sits up straighter, then seems to decide that isn't good enough and gets to his feet. He's skinny, but tall like I was at that age. I can tell he is furious with himself for getting into this situation in the first place—probably thinks he should have kept his sister safe too. I've been there.

"Tell me what happened."

He thinks about it for half a second then launches into the story. "We were playing in the woods," he repeats. "There's a game where you see who can go deepest into the woods without getting scared,"

"You were playing alone?" I ask.

He shakes his head. "There were other kids there too."

I nod. We should have interrogated the rest of the school children—they were probably afraid to admit what happened and get in trouble for being in the woods in the first place.

"And so you got lost?"

"No!" He shakes his head, and his eyes dart toward his sister.

Gwen wails louder, her tears still streaming down her face. "*I* g-g-got lost!"

"I had to go find her," Archer explains flatly.

Again, I find myself nodding. "I would have done the same thing. My sister still gets herself into all sorts of trouble."

Kastian clears his throat pointedly, but Archer doesn't seem to notice. When he answers, his tone is slightly less hostile. "Well, I found her near this house. I was mad, because she could have gotten hurt. She's too young to play that game anyway."

Gwen wails louder and Fox pats her awkwardly on the head.

"Here, eat this," Jett says, grabbing a handful of candy off a shelf and handing it to Gwen.

"Is that a good idea?" I ask sharply, eyeing the candy.

"I just ate a few of them, they're not poisoned if that's what you mean."

I nod and refocus on Archer. "You were angry, and then what?"

"I broke a window," he says flatly. "I didn't mean to. A rock just went flying out of nowhere."

Realization dawns on me, and I can suddenly picture the entire scene. They were deep in the woods, came upon the baker's house and had an argument. Archer has strong magic—that much is obvious—but it's not very well controlled, so he broke a window just like at his school.

"Did you break that barrel too?" I ask, jerking my head toward the cornmeal on the floor.

He nods. "That one was on purpose. I was trying to break the door open."

"That was smart," Kastian comments. "We wouldn't have known you were down here otherwise."

Archer almost smiles. "So when the window broke we ran up to the house and looked inside. The rock had flown inside and hit a cake. The entire town is talking about the royal wedding and we were afraid it might be the wedding cake."

Gwen, who's crying has calmed down somewhat, takes a sticky red candy out of her mouth. "We didn't want to get in trouble for ruining the wedding, and no one seemed to be home, so we went inside and...and—" she takes another shuddering breath and starts to cry again.

"—and the witch came home," Archer finishes. "She got so mad she was shaking and screaming. We tried to run away, but she caught us and threw us down here."

If I hadn't seen all the bones on the floor I would have asked if they knew why she imprisoned them, but the answer seems obvious. I find myself shaking with anger again and have to take a few more deep breaths before I can talk without scaring them.

"Alright," I grind out as calmly as possible. "Don't worry, we'll get out of here and then I'll deal with the witch...or whatever the hell she is."

"Kill her, you mean?" Archer asks.

I glance at him, weighing my answer, before deciding it's not worth lying. He might have to see it happen anyway. "Yeah."

He smiles for the first time. "Can I help?"

I snort a startled laugh. "Maybe."

"That's interesting," Kastian mutters, clearly following his own train of thought.

"What is?"

"They used magic to break a window and I can conjure a light—" he demonstrates by making a flame flicker to light in his hand "—but we can't get the door open. Maybe her spell is confined to the door itself."

"Maybe," I agree darkly. "But that doesn't help us get it open."

Jett walks around the cellar, peering at every nook and cranny. "There's a window here near the ceiling," he says after a long moment.

I spin around. "Where? I didn't see..."

My gaze lands on where he's pointing. There is in fact a small row of windows along the top of the cellar wall. They look as if they're close to ground level near the base of the foundation. At the moment, they're completely covered from the outside with snow, and from the inside they're so grimy I assumed it was just part of the stone.

"Good eyes," I admit. "Can we use magic to widen it?"

Kastian walks over, inspects the window, and gives a low whistle. "I can try, but the frame is iron."

My stomach sinks again. Iron is resistant to magic—come to think of it, maybe that's all that's going on with the door. If it's lined with iron, any magic would just bounce right off. Fucking hell.

"Excuse me," Gwen says, louder than expected. She's standing now, her chin raised, shoulders squared, eyes determined. "I can fit through it."

"No," I say, before I can stop myself.

"I can! I'm small enough."

"That's not what I meant. I meant, you can't go. It's too dangerous."

There's a ringing silence, and finally Jett breaks it. "I hate to say it, Ashwater, but it's probably our best option. Send her to the manor to get some of the soldiers. I don't doubt we can handle the baker, even if she is a witch, but unless we can get out of here..."

I wave him off, unwilling to listen to logic. "No! We can

just wait for her to open the door again. I doubt she's planning to leave us down here indefinitely."

"Why not?" Kastian asks.

I run a hand through my hair. I feel fucking stupid even this bringing it up—The Yule witch is children's story and no one truly believes in it—but I am standing in a goddamn dungeon a wall away from a room full of bones. "I think she'll have to come back down here at some point because that's how the legend goes. The Yule witch hibernates all year, and then she wakes up and she's starving, and no amount of food will satisfy her, so she steals children and eats them."

Kastian looks skeptical, but doesn't point out how absurd that sounds. "Fine, so maybe she'll come back for the kids."

"Or for all of us," Jett points out. "We'd make a better meal than a couple of kids."

"What if she doesn't come back for a few days, though." Kastian asks. "You'll miss your wedding. Everyone will think we're dead."

*Fuck.*

That's true. I can't miss the wedding or put Alix through thinking I disappeared. We can't just wait, we can't break through the door, but I also can't send a kid out into a storm. I want to fucking punch something, but I'm afraid of scaring the children.

"I'd be worried about what happens the next time that door opens." Fox says, distracting me.

I raise my eyebrows at him. "Why?"

He grinds his teeth, looking pained, but answers without much preamble. "I don't think she's just a witch. She's not even fae."

My mind is already rolling through every flavor of monster

that might want to eat children for Yule, and none of them are good. "Then what is she?"

He shakes his head hard. "I don't know. But I know how things are supposed to smell, and this house is wrong. I caught it when we first came in, but it's stronger here. It's unnatural."

Archer walks over to the window. "I might be able to squeeze through there."

I feel a hell of a lot less terrible about sending him out into the storm than the crying little girl, so I don't stop him from trying. Unfortunately, he's just slightly too big, and Fox has to yank him back out of the window so he doesn't get stuck.

"I can do it," Gwen insists. "I want to go. I'd rather be out there than in here with...*her*." Her eyes dart up to the ceiling and widen meaningfully.

I run a hand over the back of my head, squeezing my eyes shut. I can't believe I'm even considering this. "What if you get lost again?" I offer one more half-hearted protest.

"I won't," Gwen insists. "I'll follow my own footsteps back or mark the trees."

"Or leave yourself a trail," Jett suggests, picking up more brightly colored candies and handing them to her. "Just drop those behind you so you can find your way back."

She smiles widely with candy-stained teeth and nods in agreement.

8

ALIX

Between my stress about my mother and concern about the missing children, I almost forgot to panic over my wedding. *Almost.*

I eventually suggested that we all take a trip into the village to get my mother out of the house, which was when Beatrix remembered she had to stay and supervise the decorating, and Odessa reminded me that my dress still needed to be taken back to the seamstress if I wanted the final alterations finished before the wedding. I went upstairs to find the dress, and that's when all my stress came rushing back at once.

My wedding is barely a day away, and the snow is getting worse; I have no idea where Daemon is; and to make matters worse, my dress is a disaster. I swear to God, I remember Daemon being careful, but obviously "careful" wasn't enough because my beautiful, gold dress looks like crinkled old crape paper.

The grumpy seamstress is going to actually murder me. It might not even matter, because at this rate, the wedding feels cursed.

*It could be worse...right?*

Bracing myself, I gather up the dress and pile it, along with Dessa, Aurelia, Nana, and my mother, into the back of a horse-drawn sleigh. The sleigh is a bright, shiny red metal, and I chose it specifically because it reminded me of Hallmark Christmas movies, but I never pictured driving it in an actual blizzard.

"If I use magic to keep the snow off us, will your mother start screaming again?" Aurelia whispers in my ear.

I weigh the odds. "Yeah, probably...but do it anyway."

She grins and starts using her hands to direct the cold sleet away from us. She looks like she's doing some sort of interpretive dance about wind, and my mom pointedly ignores her as we set off for the village.

Our sleigh glides downhill, the runners carving twin paths through untouched snow. Spread out below us, Storia is lit up like a Christmas card, with golden windows glowing like candles in the night.

"Doesn't it look like Santa's village, Mom?" I ask over the howling wind.

My mother clutches her coat collar tight. "It's as cold as The North Pole—I'll give you that."

I roll my eyes. Due to Aurelia's dancing, it's perfectly comfortable in the sleigh, but my mom seems determined to hate everything.

We pass through the center of town and the seamstress's shop appears around the bend, its windows glowing amber against the gathering dusk. I stop the horses right outside and jump out, my crumpled dress bundled in my arms and protected from the weather by a bedsheet.

A bell jingles as I push open the door to the shop. Instead of the stern-faced woman I'd been dreading, only her assistant—a girl barely sixteen with pins stuck in her collar—looks up from behind the counter. She immediately darts out to greet me, falling into a deep curtsey. "Welcome, Your Majesty."

It's not "Your Majesty" yet, but I don't waste time correcting her. "Hi! I'm looking for Nerine?"

"I'm so sorry. Madam Nerine left an hour ago," she says, brushing a loose strand of hair from her forehead.

I bite back a groan. "Do you know where I can find her?"

"She's at the schoolhouse, fitting the children for their procession outfits—for your wedding."

"Alexandria, why are there school children in your wedding procession?"

I jump nearly a foot in the air and spin around. I hadn't noticed my mom following me inside, and now she's glaring at me with renewed suspicion.

The shop girl, clearly eager to be helpful, cuts in. "It's a royal tradition, ma'am."

"Royal?" My mother says, sounding horrified. "Who is royal?"

I put a hand over my eyes. Great. For once, I actually don't think this could get worse.

"Thank you for your help," I say begrudgingly to the assistant as I walk back out of the shop, my mother hot on my heels.

Mom peppers me with questions all the way to the new schoolhouse, until finally Nana takes pity on me and cuts in. "Iris, leave it alone. I mean it."

My mom turns her ire on her own mother instead, and I breathe a weary sigh.

Dessa pats my leg sympathetically. "Just focus on the honeypot. You're so close."

"Honeymoon," I correct her, smiling.

"Whatever. Same thing."

I shrug. "Yeah, I guess it kind of is."

We arrive at the schoolhouse and find it nearly empty, which isn't really surprising for the late hour.

A single lamp burns in the classroom at the end of the hall, casting long shadows across miniature desks. Inside, Madam Merriweather sits beside Nerine, fabric and pins scattered between them. At our entrance, Merriweather's face lights up, her chair scraping loudly as she springs upward. Nerine, however, purses her lips and slowly sets down her scissors, eyes flicking pointedly to the bundled dress in my arms like I'm carrying a bomb.

"Hi," I begin. "Sorry to bother you—"

"Not at all, Your Majesty," the teacher gushes.

Behind me, my mother's loud whisper carries throughout the room. "Alright, that's it. Is anyone going to explain the 'royalty' issue, or am I just meant to draw my own conclusions?"

"Come on, Iris," Nana sighs. "Let's go back to the carriage. I'll answer all your questions."

They leave and Madam Merriweather worries her lip, looking over my shoulder after them. "I'm sorry, was it something I said?"

"Not at all, she's just...adjusting." I grimace. "Anyway, I was actually hoping to speak with Nerine about my dress. I'm so sorry I wasn't able to finish our fitting this morning. I was wondering if there was any way you could still finish this?"

She purses her lips. "Did you sit down in it after I told you not to?"

I flush. "I mean...something like that."

She glares. "Give it to me, it's not safe with you anyway."

I hand over the dress, unsure if that means that she's going to finish it, or just that she thinks I don't deserve to wear it in the first place...probably the latter, the way things have been going today.

"I'm glad you came by," Madam Merriweather says, angling her body to block out Nerine's scowling face.

"I'm so sorry," I immediately blurt. "I know I should have come to see the children's practice for the procession earlier. I'm sure they're going to do great."

"Oh, it's not about that," she waves me off. "I haven't heard if Archer and Gwen were found yet. Did the king bring them back?"

"Actually, no. Not yet."

Her face falls. "Oh no. I hope they're all alright, it's been hours."

"You don't know Daemon or the guys, I'm sure they're fine," I say, half to convince myself as well as her. I *am* sure they're fine...but still, they've been gone much longer than I expected...

"The witch probably got them!" Nerine interrupts. "Even a king would be a fool to go after her. I bet after hibernating all year she doesn't care who she eats."

My eyes widen in alarm. "Excuse me—"

"Don't listen to her, Alix," Dessa says flatly, stepping forward to stand beside me. "This is ridiculous. There's no witch in those woods."

"Believe whatever you want," Nerine says dismissively.

"I think she's the witch," Aurelia mutters under her breath as we leave.

I laugh, but it's slightly forced. I glance up at the dark sky as we step out of the schoolhouse. "It is getting really late...when did you say they left again?"

"Right after you did," Dessa answers, her brow wrinkling slightly. "Maybe you're right. Even accounting for the weather..."

"I'm sure they're fine," I blurt out. "...but maybe we should at least check? They might want a ride back to the manor in the sleigh at the very least."

Dessa looks relieved and to my surprise, even Aurelia nods in fervent agreement.

My mother agrees to behave herself for an hour while Dessa, Aurelia, and I are gone and we drop her and Nana off at the manor before venturing out into the dark woods.

Odessa is the best with horses, having been riding most of her life, so we let her take the reins. Aurelia sits beside her, still waving her arms to keep the snow away, and I sit in the back seat feeling a little guilty that I can't do more to help.

Admittedly, if I weren't so anxious I would probably enjoy the sleigh ride.

Snow pelts the sleigh like tiny fists, but I don't feel the cold wind—just a gentle warmth radiating from where Aurelia's fingertips trace invisible patterns in the air. Twin lanterns cast yellow pools that bounce and sway ahead of us, barely penetrating the darkness. Every time we pass over a snow drift, the horses' bridle bells jingle merrily.

We ride in silence for a while but don't see any sign of the guys or any missing kids. Finally, I voice the thing I can't stop thinking about since Nerine put it in my head: "Okay, I know this sounds stupid, but I just have to ask. Is there really a Yule witch?"

Aurelia gnaws on her lip. "I mean, technically anything is possible. You can't prove she doesn't exist."

"Yes you can. I'm telling you there's no witch," Dessa says flatly. "Fae don't have that many kids. If we really lost children every single Yule there wouldn't be any left. Anyway, the word 'witch' doesn't even describe the creature in the stories."

"How so?" I ask.

"'Witch' is a human word," Aurelia explains. "Witch, sorceress, enchantress...they're all words we use to describe humans who have magic but no Fae ancestry."

"I've heard you called a sorceress before," I point out.

"My mother was one, but I'm not. I have Fae magic and trained to use it just like any other Fae."

My brow furrows. I'm certainly not the expert on Fae anything, even after living here for two years, but it's always been clear to me that Aurelia had different magic than Daemon or Kastian. I want to ask her more about it, but Dessa cuts in before I can.

"The 'Yule witch' is just a legend," Dessa insists. "But even if she was real, the creature in the stories sounds like something else to me. A shapeshifter maybe? Or some kind of hag...not that I believe she really exists."

I laugh darkly. "That doesn't make me feel better."

"Don't worry," Aurelia says. "Wouldn't you both know if

Daemon or Kastian were really in trouble? You'd feel it, right? I don't feel anything, so they're all probably fine."

"Why would *you* feel anything?" Dessa asks with a shrewd smile.

Aurelia looks startled and for a second I feel a real gust of winter air as her temperature spell falters. "I wouldn't! Not like that...I just mean I'm really good at reading people."

Dessa and I look at each other, sharing an identical suspicious look.

"Okay, that's some bullshit," I blurt out. "What did you really mean?"

Before Aurelia can answer, Dessa abruptly pulls back on the reins and the entire sleigh leaps, nearly toppling all of us into the snow.

"—the fuck!" I yell.

"Sorry!" Dessa exclaims. "I thought I saw something."

I catch myself on the side of the sleigh and peer in the direction she's pointing.

For several long moments I don't see anything except endless snow drifts and half buried trees. Then, something moves along the ground, disrupting the snow.

I gasp and reel back. Something is barreling straight at us, moving with surprising speed and utter disregard for its own safety. For one completely ridiculous second, I think it's a wolf; or worse, the witch. Then, a heavy gray blur launches itself at me.

"Sushi?" I yelp, half in disbelief, half in horror.

Nana's enormous gray cat hurls himself at the sleigh and misses entirely, rolling into a snowdrift before he lets out a yowl of such stunning volume that even the horses flinch.

"What the—" Odessa starts, but I'm already jumping off the sleigh, ignoring the way my boots fill instantly with freezing snow. I scoop up Sushi, who is, as usual, ungrateful and claws my arm for the effort.

"What the hell is wrong with you?" I scold the cat, "Go home. Go back to Nana. Why are you even here?"

The cat blinks at me with glacial, bottomless contempt in his yellow eyes. Then, like he's just remembered somewhere he needs to be, he jumps out of my grasp and bolts straight into the trees.

"God fucking dammit!"

I tear after him. My legs burn with each step through the snow, the powder spilling over my boot tops and melting against my ankles. Behind me, I hear the creak of the sleigh as Dessa and Aurelia leap down, their curses punctuating each labored breath as they follow.

Sushi's gray tail flicks back and forth over the top of the snow, taunting us as we stumble over hidden roots and sink into drifts that swallow us to mid-thigh.

"Sushi!" I yell.

"He's a cat, he's not going to come if you call him," Dessa pants.

I run around a patch of underbrush and stop short.

Sushi has stopped running and meows loudly as he stares up at me expectantly. More surprising, he's not alone.

There's a blonde little girl standing in the snow. She's pale and wild-eyed, her face streaked with tears. Sushi wraps his body around her legs, purring loudly enough that I can hear it over the wind.

"Are you Gwen?" I ask, excitement and relief flooding me.

The girl doesn't answer as without warning she hurls herself straight into my arms.

ALIX

"Is that the house?"

Gwen looks up at me and nods. She's bundled into the sleigh and looking much better now that she's safe under a pile of blankets.

It didn't take long for her to explain what happened and for us to retrace her steps back to the cottage. She hadn't been outside for very long, judging by the short length of her candy trail, and the snow hadn't yet completely covered the red sugary path. We easily found the cottage where, according to Gwen, the witch trapped them in her basement.

As soon as I get Daemon out of there and make sure he's okay I'm never going to stop making fun of him for this. He's the first person ever to have escaped the most dangerous prison in the world, but he got trapped in a root cellar by an old lady. It's too perfect.

"Stay here," I tell Gwen as I climb out of the sleigh. "We'll be right back with your brother, I promise."

"Be careful," she says in a small voice. "The witch is in there."

"I'm still not sure I believe she's a witch," Dessa mutters under her breath.

Aurelia brushes her hair back from her face and squares her shoulders. "Whatever's in there, you two should let me handle it. Stay here with Gwen, I'll go inside by myself."

I squint at her. "Are you serious?"

"No offense, but you're human, Alix, and you could get hurt. Dessa, you're not much better off than she is outside the water. Whatever's got the guys trapped in there, you should let me handle it."

I size her up, frowning. I know better than to judge fae by human standards. Aurelia is tiny and innocent looking, but in reality she's older than my nana and has absurdly powerful magic. Still, though, it's hard to look at a girl who is barely five feet tall and willingly send her off to confront a monster alone.

"What if you need help?" I hedge.

She shrugs and flashes us a slightly manic grin. "Fox, Jett, Daemon, and Kastian are in there. They'll help."

"I feel like if they could help they wouldn't be in there in the first place," I grumble. "How about you deal with the witch and we'll focus on finding and freeing the guys in case you do need backup?"

Aurelia rolls her eyes. "Fine, but at least stay behind me."

"We'll stay a few paces back," Dessa says. "Now let's go!"

We leave Gwen safely in the sleigh and creep up the path toward the tiny cottage. It looks like something out of—for lack of a better comparison—a fairytale. It's not exactly giving "evil lair" but I guess, like Aurelia, looks can be deceiving.

Right before we reach the door, Aurelia holds out her hand in the universal gesture for "wait." I don't think I've ever seen her so focused. She darts up the front steps and onto the porch, then presses her ear to the door. After a moment, she takes a step back and drives one tiny foot into the center of the door. The door shudders, then flies open with a bang and a crash of splintering wood.

"Holy shit," I breathe.

Odessa grins widely. "I've got to learn to do that."

Aurelia steps inside and we dart after her. The moment we enter the cottage I skid to a halt, my eyes going wide. My brain short-circuits, frantically recalculating.

We're standing in a cozy, one-room cottage. On one side of the room, a fire crackles in the hearth, casting dancing shadows across a flour-dusted wooden table. On the opposite side of the room, Mrs. Hilde—the baker from town—stands frozen, her spectacles slipping down her nose as she gapes at us.

In her right hand, a pastry bag drips white frosting onto her apron. In front of her, a five-tiered cake covered in delicate sugar roses teeters on the edge of the table. It looks like Mrs. Hilde bumped it with her elbow when we burst inside and, as I watch, the cake topples sideways, landing on the floor with a wet splat. Frosting splatters everywhere like arterial spray.

For a long, horrible second, I'm convinced we fucked up.

Maybe Gwen was wrong; maybe this is just a totally normal bakery emergency; maybe we just busted down the door and destroyed my second wedding cake for no reason.

I start to mouth an apology, but the words get stuck in my throat. "Mrs. Hilde? I—I'm so sorry about your door—"

But Mrs. Hilde isn't listening. Or maybe she can't.

The old lady looks from us to the cake on the floor and horror dawns on her face before morphing quickly into rage.

Her lips turn bloodless and flatten into a thin line and she lets out an anguished wail. Then, faster than I can process, her pupils dilate until her eyes are entirely black. Her jaw drops, then keeps dropping, the hinge of it distending with a nauseating, wet pop. I hear her teeth grind against each other as they grow into nightmarish fangs. Her body grows and morphs, black hair sprouting on leathery skin.

"Oh my God," I burst out. "What the fuck is that thing?"

"Stay back," Aurelia hisses, throwing her arms out to block Dessa and I from moving further into the cottage.

She doesn't have to tell me twice, I'm already scrambling back from...whatever that thing is. It—she—reminds me of a horror movie monster, like Krampus crossed with a werewolf. She's not an animal or a person, but some horrible blend of both which sends a primal terror shooting through my veins.

Unlike me, Aurelia doesn't seem afraid at all. She smiles and charges toward the thing that was Mrs. Hilde, hands outstretched.

An electric current seems to crackle in the air and of their own accord, dozens of household objects—dishes, utensils, fire tongs, and even what's left of my wedding cake—rise into the air and fly toward the monster. A sack of flour zooms off a shelf and bursts over her monstrous head, cloaking her in a blizzard of white dust. For a moment, she's blinded and furious, shrieking as the flour clings to every grotesque crevice of her face.

Mrs. Hilde bellows a horrible roar that rattles the entire cottage and lunges after Aurelia. Aurelia darts out of the way and avoids being clawed but manages to slip on the frosting-covered floor and lose her balance. She scrambles across the floor and the monster lumbers after her.

Completely ignoring Aurelia's instructions to hang back,

Dessa grabs a rolling pin off the table and swings it like a base-ball bat at Mrs. Hilde's head.

She misses her target, but still manages to connect with the creature's huge, hairy shoulder. A resounding crack rattles through the cabin and Mrs. Hilde roars in pain and rage.

Dessa grins, but her excitement is short lived. The monster swipes its injured arm toward Dessa, grabbing her by the throat and lifting her effortlessly, fingers tightening, squeezing so hard Dessa's feet dangle off the ground.

I scream out of sheer terror, and to my surprise Mrs. Hilde stops shaking Dessa to look at me. Our gazes connect and she abruptly drops Dessa and changes direction, charging toward the next closest intruder—me.

"She can't focus on all of us at once!" Aurelia yells behind me, having clearly had the same realization I just did.

Not that that knowledge helps me at all as I shriek and try to jump out of the way of the charging creature. My human reflexes are too slow and Mrs. Hilde swipes at me with enor-mous claws and I close my eyes just before I feel a hand shoving me out of the way.

I land hard against the wall and my vision blurs as Aurelia jumps in front of me. I blink in surprise when I see her wings are out.

I've never seen Aurelia's wings before—or any female fae's wings for that matter. They're smaller than any other fae wings I've seen and are an electric blueish-green like a hummingbird.

I blink, dazed for half a second, before a loud bang and shouting jogs my attention.

I look around frantically for the source of the sound, my eyes landing on a door on the far wall. Oh fuck, the guys must be in there.

I stay on my hands and knees and crawl across the frosting-covered floor, wincing every time a shadow passes over me or the monster roars.

I reach the other side of the room and pull myself up on the door handle. It's locked from the outside, but luckily the key is still shoved into the lock. I turn it and yank the door open.

Immediately, four large men and a boy come spilling out. If the cottage felt small before, now it's suffocating. Daemon, Kastian, Fox, and Jett all have their wings out, and their wingspans are far larger than Aurelia's. Between the eight bodies, five sets of wings, and one rampaging baker, there's barely room to breathe.

Daemon grabs me roughly by the upper arms and shoves me back against the wall, shielding me with his body. My heart leaps when I lock eyes with Daemon, but he doesn't look at all happy to see me. He grips me by the arms and hauls me behind him, practically suffocating me against the wall.

"What are you doing here?" he roars over the sounds of continued fighting.

"I could ask you the same thing!" I shout back. "You're welcome by the way!"

He looks like he's not sure if he wants to strangle me or kiss me, and winds up pushing me further behind him as he turns to face the fight.

I peer around his red and brown wing, and find that the fight is nearly over.

Dessa, bruised but back in the fight, swings the rolling pin at Mrs. Hilde's head with a yell, just before Kastian reaches her. He doesn't even waste his time on the monster, just grabs his bond and picks her up. She yells in protest as he carries her kicking out of the house.

Aurelia plants her feet wide, arms raised overhead. The air

around her fingers crackles and pops, tiny blue-white arcs jumping between her knuckles. Before she can unleash whatever's building in her palms, Fox lunges between her and Mrs. Hilde.

His towering height and huge muscles cast Aurelia in shadow and put him nearly at eye level with the snarling beast. He snarls back before he throws his full weight forward, slamming Mrs. Hilde into the flour-covered floor. Fox's muscles strain, veins popping in his forearms as he pins Mrs. Hilde's thrashing body to the ground.

Then a blur of movement catches my eye—Archer, darts out of nowhere, his face set in grim determination, fingers white-knuckled around the wooden handle of a serrated bread knife that looks massive in his small hands. Without hesitation, he drives the knife down into the monster's chest and a wet, gurgling sound fills the cottage as dark liquid spurts across Archer's trembling fingers.

ALIX

After the battle with the "Yule witch" we all returned to the manor, albeit in waves.

Kastian and Odessa were the first to make it home because he literally picked her up, walked out of the cabin, and didn't stop walking until they were safely back in the manor. Of course she's livid about being dragged out of the fight against her will, but I think she's secretly glad that his priorities are so clear.

Fox, Jett, and Aurelia returned home next. It's not entirely clear what happened between leaving the cabin and arriving at the manor an hour later, but Dessa told me that the mood was tense when they arrived and Fox was even more quiet than usual.

Finally, Daemon and I were last. We decided to bring Archer and Gwen back to Nikolas ourselves, both because this was technically part of our traditional wish granting and we wanted to make sure to fully complete our mission, but mostly because we felt it was important to explain exactly how and why Gwen had been sent out into the storm alone and how Archer managed to murder the monster. To our relief, Nikolas was so grateful to see his grandchildren that the details weren't important.

"How can I ever repay you?" he cries when we've finished explaining what happened.

"We don't need anything," Daemon says immediately. "It was part of the traditional wish granting."

"And even if it weren't we still would have helped." I add.

Daemon nods. "That too."

Nikolas hugs his grandchildren, one in each arm, tears pouring down his face. "Surely there's something I can do."

Daemon starts to wave him off again, then stops. "Actually..."

I glance at him sharply. "You're not seriously—"

"No," he says quickly, "It's not a repayment, I was just curious. Who's tutoring the children in magic?"

Nikolas shakes his head and Archer is the one to answer. "No one. Our parents used to teach us, but now no one does. There aren't that many magic users in Storia."

"Yes there are, they just all live on our estate with us," Daemon says. "If you were interested in continuing to train your magic, I could teach you."

"You?" Nikolas says, awed.

"Well, me and whoever else was around to give lessons."

Archer and Gwen sit up straighter, both looking excited, but their grandfather interrupts.

"That's far too generous," Nikolas says quickly. "And surely you wouldn't have the time while running the country."

Daemon shrugs. "Just think about it. We can talk about it more after we get back from our honeymoon."

Nikolas doesn't seem to know what a honeymoon is, but he's too polite to ask. He thanks us again and we leave, stepping out into the dark, snowy street. The moment the door closes behind us I turn to Daemon. "That was a generous offer. Do you really have time to teach them?"

He shrugs. "I'll make time. Aurelia will help, and Kastian, when he's on land. We can send Archer to Fox too. That lad's got killer instincts and he's old enough to be a squire."

"I guess, but it was still a big favor to offer spontaneously. Not that I mind, I'm just curious."

"I'm shit at talking to kids, but I'll have to learn eventually, right? This will be good practice."

The corner of my mouth pulls up in a smile. "You're thinking we'll have kids soon?"

He shrugs. "Maybe. I'm ready whenever you are, Peaches. Anyway, that wasn't the only reason I offered to train them. We're a new country and we're still building up our powerbase. We could use two magic users who are brave enough to walk out into a storm alone or stab a witch...or whatever the hell that thing was."

"You don't know? That was going to be my next question. What was she?"

He frowns. "I don't know, Peaches. There are lots of creatures in Ellender that are far older and more dangerous than the Fae. I know one thing, though: the next time I hear one of those old children's legends, I'll assume it's real until proven otherwise."

"That's probably a good strategy. I mean, my favorite stories turned out to be real too—" I gesture around at the street around us "—so clearly there's precedent."

Daemon grins and kisses me hard on the mouth. We don't break apart for several long seconds until finally I smile against his lips. "What was that for?"

"Just wanted to remind you that I love you before I spend the entire way home reminding you how fucking dangerous it was to come looking for us."

"Oh please. Without Aurelia, Dessa, and me you would all still be stuck in the basement."

He growls. "Don't remind me. I don't want to think about how she managed to trap all of us so easily and I especially don't want to think of what could have happened to you."

I grin. "Then don't. Let's just go home. As unbelievable as it is, we still have tons of shit to do before the wedding... assuming it doesn't get snowed out."

"Even if it does, we're still going on our honeymoon," he grumbles.

I nod fervently. "Of course, I—oh shit!"

Daemon furrows his brow. "What's wrong?"

"I just remembered I have to tell you something. My mother is here and she's been dying to meet you. I'd brace yourself, this could be rough."

He sighs and grabs my hand. "Alright. Come on Peaches, let's get this over with."


A few hours later, Daemon, and I sit on a couch by a roaring fire in the middle of our sitting room. Christmas music emanates from my battery-operated CD player—the only way I can play human music in Ellender— and the scent of freshly baked cookies wafts in from the kitchen. Around us, the entire room is packed to bursting, and every seat is full.

My mom, who warmed up to Daemon immediately upon realizing that he's gorgeous and literally a king, is sitting in an armchair to our right and smiling. I haven't seen her so serene in years and it's honestly creeping me out.

Nana sits in another armchair beside Mom, chatting with Beatrix while Sushi snoozes on her lap. I don't know when Sushi found his way back to the manor, but I guess I can't complain that he was out in the woods after he led us straight to Gwen. I swear that cat is smarter than he should be.

On the other side of the room, Dessa and Kastian are sitting on the floor, grinning as they watch Jett and Connell drag Aurelia around the room, passing her back and forth in something resembling a three-person waltz.

Fox leans against the wall, his arms crossed, also watching the dancing. His expression is completely unreadable, but his light eyes keep flicking to Aurelia, then looking away the moment she turns in his direction. *Interesting.*

I sigh contentedly and lean back against Daemon's chest. He reaches up absently and drags his fingers through my hair. "You okay, Peaches?"

I nod. "Great, actually. This would be a perfect evening, except for the storm."

Daemon glances at the dark window where the snow is still raging on.

Beatrix, clearly overhearing us, raises her voice to be heard over the music. "Don't worry, Alix, the wedding guests will still make it."

I sigh. "I appreciate the optimism, but I'm not so sure. We might have to accept that the other courts aren't going to be able to get here in time."

"All the fucking better," Daemon growls. "I keep telling

you, we're bonded. We don't need to put on a show in front of a thousand strangers."

I pat his arm affectionately. "I know. Honestly, I'd be happy to get married right this second with only you all here."

There's a ringing silence throughout the room where only the slightly scratchy sounds of *Walking in a Winter Wonderland* play out of the boombox.

"Then why don't you?" Jett says finally.

"What, get married right now?"

"Ooh yes," Dessa gushes, sitting up straighter. "You should."

I laugh. "But we've been planning this huge thing for months."

Beatrix and my nana glance at each other, then at me.

"I think that big ship has sailed, Ali," Nana says. "All the optimism in the damn world won't change the weather."

My heart starts to beat a little faster, excitement and anticipation building in my gut. I crane my neck to look at Daemon. "What do you think?"

He grins at me. "I like it."

"Ooh, okay!" Dessa jumps up, clapping her hands together. "That's settled then. Alix, come on, I'll help you get ready."

I smile back and start to rise, then my stomach sinks. "No, wait. Nerine still has my dress, and honestly I don't know how willing she'll be to give it back. That woman seems as obsessed with her sewing as Mrs. Hilde was with her baking. I'm afraid if I wrinkle the dress again she'll turn into another one of those Krampus-looking nightmares."

Everyone laughs, but I'm not entirely joking. Maybe we should double check there aren't more of those monstrous old ladies wandering around...after we get back from our honeymoon, that is.

"You could always wear my dress, Alixandrea," my mom says loftily.

I look over at her. "Mom...even if I wanted to, it's not here."

"Actually, it is."

I stare at her, bemused, until finally it clicks. "You packed the dress to bring to 'Ireland,' didn't you?"

Mom doesn't look the least bit abashed. "I might not have if I'd known I'd be shoved in a lake. You're lucky I always triple wrap everything in space-saver bags when I travel or it would have been ruined."

"Not to sway your decision, Ali," Nana pipes up, "But am I to understand you have to grant any wish in the week leading up to your wedding?"

"Yeah, but we only had to grant a thousand and we just finished that today."

"Actually," Daemon begins slowly. "We had 998 wishes granted this morning, Peaches. Rescuing the kids made 999, but there's still one left."

My eyes widen and I try to think back to all the other wishes we granted this week...he's right.

I turn to my mom. "Is this really important to you?"

She nods once. "I clearly don't know anything about your life, Alixandrea—I mean, Alix—" she corrects herself, using my preferred name for the first time in living memory. "I just want to be included."

My heart melts just a little. "Okay, then let's do it."

My mom beams.

Daemon and I get married at midnight in the rose garden behind our house.

Aurelia bends the weather just slightly to keep the snow from piling up on us and our guests. Even though I'd assumed that only our closest friends and family would witness our impromptu wedding, we actually have a far larger audience.

The garden fills with whispers and shuffling feet as the now familiar faces of all the soldiers, servants, and townspeople who we've been granting wishes for all week crowd into the garden dressed in heavy coats thrown hastily over nightclothes.

Standing in front of the pond, moonlight catches on the brass buttons of Kastian's, Fox's, and Jett's matching navy jackets, their shoulders straight as they flank Daemon. The crowd hushes as Aurelia and Dessa walk toward them down the makeshift aisle, bunches of roses in their hands, their golden dresses shimmering with each step.

My nana's fingers tremble slightly against my right arm, my mother's grip firm on my left as we step forward. The white lace of Mom's dress catches on the frozen rosebushes, tiny crystals of ice clinging to the hem with each step.

Behind me, Gwen whispers "Careful!" to Archer as they guide the other children holding my train off the ground.

I look up and lock eyes with Daemon. His pupils dilate in the moonlight, and the corner of his mouth lifts in that half-smile that still makes my heart stutter.

When we finally reach the front of the crowd, my mom's fingers slip away from my arm, and Nana gives me one last, surreptitious squeeze before releasing me.

Daemon catches my hand immediately—like he's been waiting to do it all his life—and grins down at me with a look that's so unguarded, so him, that for a second the crowd's whispers fade to silence and it's as if we're all alone.

The fae priest is not what I expected. He's shorter than Aurelia and wears a robe the color of fresh moss with a dusting of snow on the shoulders. His eyes are sharp but his smile is enormous and takes up most of his face when he greets us. He holds a golden rope in his hands, the ends knotted with little blue and white beads that glitter like frost, and gestures for Daemon and I to clasp our hands together.

"Friends, citizens, and honored guests," he begins, his voice somehow both musical and gravelly. "We gather under the old moon and the new snow to witness the joining of these two souls."

Somebody—probably Jett—whistles. I can't help but grin.

The priest gestures again and Daemon and I step closer, our hands now firmly joined. The priest begins winding the rope around our wrists, the gold and beads cold and heavy against my skin. Each loop is punctuated with a question: "Do you come here freely?"

"Yes."

"Do you bind your fate together, for better or worse?"

"It could always be worse," I mutter automatically.

Daemon laughs.

The vows are long and traditional and punctuated by many sniffles from the crowd. It's possible I'm crying too, I can't tell because my nose is numb and my eyes are watery from the cold, but my heart is about to trampoline out of my chest. I try to collect myself, but all I can think is how much I love this man and how lucky I am that I found my way here to this very moment.

When the priest's weathered fingers secure the final knot with practiced precision, the golden cord wraps halfway up our wrists. The priest's eyes crinkle at the corners as he steps back.

"May your fates be tangled together forever," he says, voice carrying across the hushed garden. "You may kiss."

Daemon's free hand finds the small of my back, pulling me closer until our breath mingles in the cold air between us. When our lips finally meet, the crowd erupts: Jett and Kastian whooping at the top of their lungs, Beatrix sobbing, Nana cheering, and even my mother quietly blows her nose.

Daemon pulls back, his lips still warm against the shell of my ear. "I love you, Peaches," he whispers, the words a secret between us despite the hundred witnesses. My cheeks ache from smiling as our bound hands swing between us and we walk back down the aisle and into our happily ever after.

DAEMON

I carry my wife over the threshold into our bedroom and kick the door shut behind us.

I'd planned to bring Alix on a tour of Ellender so she could see all the other countries she hasn't yet had time to visit. We were supposed to leave for Solistine right after the wedding, but the snow made it impossible.

"Are you disappointed to spend your wedding night in our normal room?" I ask as I carry her over to the bed.

She laughs, running her smiling lips along my jaw. "I don't have the ability to be disappointed about anything right now. We could spend all of the next two weeks in this room and I'd be thrilled."

I grin and put her down on the edge of the bed. "Glad you say that, Peaches, because it looks like we might have to."

She glances at the window and we're both silent for a

moment, listening to the howling wind and the snow pelting the glass. Alix turns back to me and grins wider. "Sounds perfect."

She wraps her arms around my neck and pulls me down for a kiss. I moan into her mouth, feeling my cock grow hard against her. "If I'm not inside you in the next five seconds I'm going to fucking die."

She pulls back a fraction, her mouth hovering a breath away from mine. "I feel like I'm going to die if I don't get a bath after such a long day. Maybe we can kill two birds?"

My lips curl up as I bend to scoop her into my arms. Her thighs tighten around me, the silk of her wedding dress rustling between us as I navigate around the four-poster bed and stride toward our adjoining bathing room.

I put Alix down on the edge of the enormous porcelain tub and lean over to turn on the faucets. The roar of water fills the room.

While we wait for the bath to fill, Alix stands up and steps around me. She reaches behind her back and tugs down the zipper of her white lace dress. "That's the next thing I'm going to make sure we get in Ellender."

"What?" I ask, blinking rapidly as she steps out of the pool of white fabric, leaving the dress on the tiled floor.

Alix smirks. "Zippers. Much easier access than corsets."

Alix saunters toward me, the white lace of her undergarments stark against her flushed skin. She closes the distance between us until I feel the heat of her body through my clothes. I catch her by the waist as she rises on her toes, her mouth trailing up my throat. Her fingers work at my jacket, peeling it away as she presses herself against me. My cock grows even harder between us and I growl against her mouth.

Alix pulls back, her gaze flicking to the half-full tub behind me. The corner of her mouth lifts, eyes darkening as she holds my stare. I don't know what she's thinking until she sinks onto her knees in front of me and I almost choke on my own tongue.

The sight of her kneeling, half dressed, hair falling in soft waves over bare shoulders, her hands trailing lightly down my hips, is enough to short-circuit my nervous system. The air in the room seems to grow thin. My heart is pounding so hard I'm sure she can hear it over the rush of water.

She looks up at me through her lashes, the faintest smirk tugging at the corner of her mouth. She reaches up slowly, deliberately—drawing it out, making me feel every single millimeter of anticipation—and undoes my belt with a single practiced motion. She makes a mischievous purr in the back of her throat that shoots straight to my cock. I groan audibly, which only seems to amuse her more.

Alix slips my belt from the loops and drapes it over her shoulder like a sash of honor, then starts on the button of my trousers. Her knuckles brush my abdomen, and I tense involuntarily—my entire body humming under her touch. My shirt is still on, but her hands glide beneath the hem, hunting for bare skin. Her nails scrape lightly over my hips, making me shudder.

She tugs open the rest of the buttons on my trousers and my cock springs free, hard enough that it aches. She runs her fingers lightly along my shaft, teasing, exploring.

She wraps her hand around the base of my cock, then rocks forward on her knees. She kisses the head, slow and deliberate, then she licks a stripe up the underside, circling back to the tip with a wickedly talented tongue. I groan, and my knees threaten to buckle.

I hiss and brace one hand against the marble wall, the other tangled in her hair, barely restraining myself from thrusting into her mouth the second she flicks her tongue out to taste me.

I'm suddenly starving for her—ravenous in a way that feels a little dangerous. I reach down and pull her hair to get her attention. "Look at me."

She does. Her blue eyes flick up to mine, as she takes me back into her mouth, inch by excruciating inch, and the world narrows to the wet heat and the way her throat vibrates when she hums in satisfaction.

She sets a rhythm, one hand wrapping tight around my base, the other cradling my hip. I let my head fall back and close my eyes, but after a minute, I can't take it anymore. If she keeps doing that I'm coming down her throat, and that's not what I want right now.

Alix makes a noise of protest as I haul her to her feet and kiss her like I might never get the chance again. Her body arches into mine, soft and yielding and impossibly warm.

She's flushed all the way down her neck, eyes bright with mischief. Then, as if making a show of it, she peels off her ridiculous lace underwear, careful and slow, letting the fabric snag over her thighs before tossing it to the floor.

I don't even get a second to appreciate the view before she's climbing over the lip of the tub, one leg at a time, pale skin ghosting against the sharp white porcelain. I fumble my shirt off, too frantic to bother with the buttons and just tugging it over my head, then nearly moan at the sight of Alix already sinking into the water, naked and wet, lips parted in invitation.

The tub is comically oversized, ornate, with gold fixtures and enough room for three people. I sink against the back of it, stretching my legs, and she settles between them, her back pressed to my chest. I wrap my arms around her, hands roaming up her slick stomach to cup her breasts, thumbs circling over the peaks. She gasps, arching into my touch.

She turns her head to kiss me, slow at first, then hungry, her tongue gliding against mine as her hands reach behind her, gripping my thighs. I trace my fingers down her stomach, over her hip bones, and she lets out a sound that borders on a whimper when my fingers trace over her folds. Her head falls back against my shoulder, her breath catching in her throat as my fingers find that sensitive spot where she's already slick and swollen.

I take my time exploring her, feeling her pulse quicken beneath my touch as I drag my fingers over her slowly, circling her clit in lazy teasing strokes. She moans, low and desperate, the sound echoing off the marble walls. I slide my free hand up to her jaw and press my thumb against her fluttering pulse.

She whimpers and rocks back into me, greedy for friction, her ass grinding against my cock under the water. I can't resist —I stop stroking her just long enough to reach down and guide myself between her ass cheeks letting the swollen tip nudge against her.

Alix parts her thighs wider, the motion sending little ripples across the surface of the bath, and I slide my hand between her legs again, this time with far less restraint. She's so sensitive I can feel every tremor under my fingertips as I work steady, deliberate circles over her clit, picking up speed and pressure.

She digs her nails into my thighs for leverage, grinding back against my cock so the head slips back and forth between her cheeks, caught in the tight grip of her body and the warm swirl of the water. Her skin is flushed everywhere—cheeks, neck, chest, the little line of her jaw where she keeps biting herself to stay quiet. I want to tell her not to bother, that she could scream the damn roof down and I'd be proud, but I'm not sure I can form actual words.

I keep my rhythm tight and relentless, my other hand moving from her throat to splay across her pelvis and hold her in place while I work her over with my fingers. She starts to shiver, first just in her thighs, then her whole body, and her voice shatters in a single sharp moan.

The sight and sound of it is almost enough to finish me, but I'm greedy for her, so I double down, slowing my touch just enough to draw it out, keeping her perched in that sweet spot between agony and bliss. She's shaking so hard I have to wrap an arm across her ribcage to keep her from sliding under the water.

Finally, she bucks against me and wrenches my wrist in a silent plea for mercy. I let go and she collapses back against my chest, boneless and half-laughing, the kind of laughter that's pure relief.

When she's recovered somewhat, Alix twists around in my arms, shifting so she's straddling my lap, knees braced on the smooth bottom of the tub. The water rises to her chest, beads rolling down her skin. She presses her forehead to mine, gaze locked, and then lines herself up and sinks onto me in one slow, agonizing glide.

The heat, the wet, the sheer fucking tightness of her—it's all I can do not to lose it on the spot. I grip her hips, holding her steady as she starts to move, rolling her body with a practiced rhythm that makes the whole world go white around the edges.

She tangles her hands in my hair as she kisses me deeper.

I grip her hips, guiding her up and down. I can barely breathe. The pressure is building, every nerve in my body focused on where we're joined, and she's whispering my name over and over, losing words as she starts to fall apart.

"Fuck—Alix—" I choke out, and before the words are fully formed, her entire body goes taut. She arches back with a strangled gasp, her fingers clawing at my shoulders for purchase. She bites down hard on my neck as the ripple of her orgasm pulses through her and into me.

The feeling of her clenching around me is so intense that there's no chance of holding back. I hear myself make a guttural sound and I lock my arms around her, crushing her to my chest and come hard, the climax ripping through me with enough force to blur my vision.

She doesn't let go. She plants her hands on either side of my face, forehead pressed to mine and I hold her there, locked in place and I don't let her move, not even an inch, not until I'm sure she's taken every drop. Only then do I loosen my grip, just enough that she can collapse against me, limp and spent, her arms wrapped around my neck and her heart thumping double-time against my ribs.

Alix shifts and tries to stand, but I grab her hips and hold her down. "Where do you think you're going?"

She blinks at me. "Uh, I don't know. Maybe to grab a towel?"

I shake my head and hold her closer. "Don't even fucking think about it. You're not going anywhere for the next two weeks."

She laughs. "We're going to have to at least pause to eat."

I shake my head again, though I'm smiling now. "We're immortal, Peaches. Technically, we don't *have* to eat."

Her brow wrinkles. "Are you sure about that?"

"No, but I'm willing to test it." I grin and press my lips to the curve of her throat. "I have much more important things to do with my mouth."

She laughs and throws her head back. "I guess it could be worse."

# ABOUT THE AUTHOR

USA Today and International bestselling author Kate King loves sassy heroines, crazy magic, and alpha-hole heroes.

An avid reader and writer from a young age, she has been telling stories her whole life. Ever a fan of the dramatic, she lives in an 18th century church with her husband and two cats, and often writes in cemeteries.